"A lot of women come looking for a man."

Neil's thumb pressed Serena's jaw, urging her eyes to his. "They aren't interested in a crewing job."

"I'm not looking for a man." It seemed like a lie, because when he touched her she felt like a woman waiting for her lover. "I came—I—this is the year that I would have been going to the South Pacific but—" The sad failure of Terry's dreams trembled on her lips but something in his eyes stopped her.

"Some men come looking for crew," he told her harshly. "Some are looking for a woman." He was frowning.

"And is that why you came?" she breathed.

"I came for crew. But—" his fingers pressed her arm, "if you are looking for a man," he said oddly, "I've a feeling it had better be me."

Vanessa Grant started writing her first romance at the age of twelve and hasn't forgotten the excitement of having a love story come to life on paper. After spending almost four years refitting the forty-six-foot yacht they live on, she and her husband have set sail with their teenage son to cruise south to Mexico along the North American west coast. Vanessa divides her time between her writing, sailing and exploring the harbors of the Pacific coast. She has her own special place on the boat that Brian has outfitted as her office, and she often works on her love stories on her portable computer while anchored in remote inlets. Vanessa says, "I believe in love and in happy endings."

Books by Vanessa Grant

HARLEQUIN PRESENTS
895—STORM
1088—JENNY'S TURN
1112—STRAY LADY
1179—TAKEOVER MAN
1209—STRANDED HEART
1234—AWAKENING DREAMS

HARLEQUIN ROMANCE
2888—THE CHAUVINIST

VANESSA GRANT

wild passage

Harlequin Books

TORONTO • NEW YORK • LONDON
AMSTERDAM • PARIS • SYDNEY • HAMBURG
STOCKHOLM • ATHENS • TOKYO • MILAN

This one is for Brian
for blending love and adventure

Harlequin Presents first edition May 1990
ISBN 0-373-11264-5

Original hardcover edition published in 1989
by Mills & Boon Limited

CHAPTER ONE

IT WAS like no other party she had ever seen.

Serena stood at the open door, suddenly wary of entering. Inside was a rough room, a waterfront warehouse hardly decorated, filled with hundreds of people, their voices raised in passionate, discordant conversation. No music, only a wild press of people dressed in everything from casual to downright scruffy. Jeans. Mexican ponchos. Fishermen's rain slickers. Over the heads of the crowd she could see inflatable boats hanging from the ceiling. On the walls—boat ladders, flare kits, rain slickers and twisted, shiny pieces of metal she could not begin to identify.

She was probably the only woman in the place wearing a dress. Thankfully, she had worn casual shoes instead of high heels, and her wild brown curls were always casual.

'Which?' shouted a girl with a metal cash-box. The girl was seated behind a collapsible table that had probably been borrowed from the school across the street. She might have been collecting admissions for a charity benefit, but the noise level ruled out anything so civilised. A bearded, overly muscled man came parading past with a painted sign held casually in his arm—'Wanted! Crew'.

Serena knew she did not belong here, would never have come if today were not the first day of August.

'Which are you?' shouted the girl insistently, her long black hair sweeping over the record book in front of her, her fingers hovering over the money. 'Hurry up! You're blocking the line.'

'No, I——' She drew back, came up hard against a solid, broad chest, could feel the heat of a male body. If it had happened on a bus or in a crowded hallway, she would have moved unobtrusively without looking, breaking contact without acknowledging it. But here, tense, she jerked around fast, her face giving away her confusion even in the half-light.

'Sorry.' His strong, deep voice reinforced an impression of hard muscles and overwhelming maleness.

'My fault,' she gasped. Unruly blond hair, dark eyes. Strength. How old was he? Thirty? Forty? Old enough to have developed deep lines of character on his face. He was wearing tight-fitting jeans and a T-shirt that advertised a marina in Mexico. A sailor. Heavy biceps stretching the shirt. She swallowed, fighting an oddly sensual vision of this man pulling hard on the halyard of a big mainsail, his arms raised over his head to grip the line, his thighs bulging as he braced his legs on the deck.

She stepped back quickly, flustered by the unexpected impact he made on her. Her relationship with her husband had been warm and pleasant, with none of the panicky heat she could feel right now. Hadn't she read somewhere that women became more sensual as they get older? That must be it. She was nearing thirty and this was certainly a sensual feeling.

He was a total stranger, yet he had the flavour of an old, close, exciting friend as he smiled and explained, 'I thought you were going in, like everyone else,' and she found herself smiling back at him, wondering where she might have seen him before, almost wishing he were someone she would see again.

'Well?' demanded the cash-box girl. 'Which? Pink dot is for crew. Blue dot is for boat owners.'

'Blue,' said the deep-toned voice behind her.

'Registered?' The long-haired girl was happy to give up on Serena for someone who knew what he was doing.

'Yup. Neil Turner.' He leaned across the table and placed a darkly tanned finger beside a name on the girl's list. 'There. *Passagemaker.*' That muscled hand belonged to the kind of man who knew exactly what he wanted, and got it.

Inside, someone screamed a greeting. Someone else laughed. The roar of conversation surged up and flowed through the door. To Serena it seemed the noise was pounding in her chest, as if her heart were going crazy. She pushed a worried hand through her short brown curls. When she was under the sun, her hair glistened with an enticing copper shade, but now in the dim light it seemed to match her dark eyes.

The girl behind the table reached past with a piece of paper bearing a blue dot, as if Serena were not even there. Serena glanced back and saw Neil Turner slapping the sticky label on to his shirt, right over the picture of a boat at dock. His name had been printed on the label by computer, and the name of his boat. So he was expected here, and she did not belong, yet his eyes held hers for long seconds until she could almost believe he would touch her elbow and she would follow him into that mob.

It made no sense at all, but she would remember his name when winter came. He would be somewhere exotic, she supposed, while she stayed right here in British Columbia, trying to persuade a class of students that French was a language worth learning. She loved teaching, but the same school, the same classes and the last six years seemed like forever as she looked into a man's dark eyes, eyes that had seen the world.

'Thanks, love,' said the man, his voice too close, his words for the black-haired girl. Serena looked away, then back, and found with a shock that his eyes were still on her, eyes as dark as her own. Too obviously virile. Too aware of his attraction. A strong man. The kind you wanted around in an emergency. How long since she had felt this excitement? Had she ever felt quite this?

Then he was gone, and she was abruptly facing the cash-box and the collapsible table again. 'What are you looking for? A boat or a crew?' The girl behind the table was losing patience with Serena as several new people pressed close, seeking admission to the chaos inside. A man in a Greek fisherman's cap shouted, 'Hey, let's move it!'

'I'm not registered,' Serena said hurriedly, easing back towards the door. 'I——'

'Doesn't matter.' The girl's voice was almost kind now. 'Do you have a boat?' Serena shook her head. 'OK. Looking to crew.' Her manicured fingers peeled a pink dot from a sheet filled with them. 'Five dollars if you're not registered.'

She found her fingers fumbling for the money. 'Five dollars,' repeated the woman, slapping the dot on to a blank identification label. 'Put your name on this and wear it.'

She didn't belong, but ever since that afternoon when she saw the poster in the window of the marine store she had felt the pull.

'Kick-off party for cruisers sailing to Mexico and the

South Pacific. Whether you're looking for crew, or looking for a boat to crew on, this is the party for you.'

How could she resist? It had been such a long, uncomfortably idle summer. Last summer had been filled with losing Terry. This one was empty, endless. Terry's dream had drawn her here, because this was the first day of August. She moved slowly through the crowd, stumbled against a rubber dinghy right in the middle of all those people. It was filled with ice and cans of soft drinks.

'Hey!' She turned around and found herself staring at a very young, smoothly handsome man. He was holding a paper cup in either hand. 'Here! I can't find the guy I was getting this for. You may as well have it.'

The crowd shifted. She was now part of a group of five who were shouting to hear each other. She lifted the paper cup which had been pushed into her hand and sipped, tried to look as if she belonged without attracting any questions to herself. A cool wine slipped down her throat.

'You looking for a crew job to where?' The man beside her had turned, setting himself apart from the others. 'Where do you want to go? I'm headed for the South Pacific. Hawaii, then the South Pacific.'

She shook her head. 'No, I——'

'Hawaii, even,' he said, smiling at her. 'If you only want to go to Hawaii, that's fine. I can find someone else over there.'

'No, I'm not really—I just want to go down the coast. Excuse me.' She stepped back, saying, 'I think the fellow over there wanted to go to the South Pacific.'

'Which one?' He twisted his neck to look. 'The guy with the purple shirt?'

'Yes,' she agreed quickly. People everywhere. Noise everywhere. She had no idea where she was going, but she kept moving, listening, her mind in a daze.

'. . . so I put up the spinnaker and pulled away from him, like' . . . 'gale warning, but the fool went out anyway. So, of course he was blown back into' . . . 'his wife wouldn't set foot on the boat, so he left her and went sailing' . . . 'can't make up my mind between the Hood furling main and' . . . 'crewed on this sixty-foot ketch, but the captain was a pig and I jumped ship at San Francisco. I heard the next crew he took on did the same' . . . 'shipwrecked off the coast of Africa. They worked for two years to rebuild the boat, then took her out and finished the trip' . . . 'started out with three hundred dollars and came back five years later with five hundred.'

She felt him watching her, would not look, but the tension built. It was as if he were willing her to turn and smile at him. She told herself it was imagination, but when she turned he was there. The man with the marina shirt. Under the bright overhead light he looked closer to forty than thirty. His face was darkly tanned, the paler flesh around his eyes hinting that he usually wore sunglasses. He was standing with a couple dressed in matching red jogging outfits. The colour contrasted horribly with the woman's brightly dyed hair.

'—dreamed of it all our lives,' the woman was saying, 'but we thought we'd better try it first. That makes sense, doesn't it? To find out if we like sailing before we spend all that money on a boat?' It made sense to Serena, but she felt almost as if she could read the mind of the darkly tanned man. Somehow, this couple would be trouble, not help on board his boat.

Neil. She practised his name in her mind, feeling the

unfamiliar excitement of knowing he would seek her out before the evening was over. She sipped the wine again. Had she drunk the whole cupful? She must have, because the cup was empty. She looked for a place to put the empty cup, but there was nowhere.

'Give me your name and phone number,' she heard him saying smoothly, but knew that he would never call them. His eyes met Serena's and she saw his lips twitch in a suppressed smile, as if he knew what she sensed. Then he was moving, coming closer with a look in his eyes that sorted her out from the rest of the crowd.

She looked for somewhere to run, but the people were pressed hard against her: loud, excited people who did not move easily when she pushed for a corridor out of this confusion.

'Neil! Good heavens, Neil! I haven't seen you in a hundred years. Where have you been since Tahiti?' She saw his head lift at the sound of his name, then he was holding an armful of beautiful woman with long blonde hair, murmuring something in a low voice that Serena could not hear.

She turned away quickly, her hand going to her own short curls. He had called the long-haired cash-box girl 'love' and this one was in his arms. He liked his women with long, sleek hair. She felt the old yearning of her teenage years for the romantic sweep of a beautiful head of long, sexy hair. Silly! Her one attempt to grow her hair had proven forever that her full, broad cheekbones looked wrong with anything but short, curly locks of windblown hair.

He was a stranger. A husky, sexy man she would never see again, did not want to see again.

'Looking for a boat to crew on?' The woman seemed to pop out of the crowd, her voice low and friendly, face

round and smiling. 'My husband and I are sailing to
Mexico alone.'

'I—are you?' She looked back and found the man
named Neil. His arm was loosely around the blonde
girl's waist, his head bent to hear her words. Was
everyone in the world paired in twos? Everyone but
Serena Jones?

'Yes. We want to——Oh, good!' The name on the
woman's label was Hilda, and she pounced on a man
carrying a tray full of paper cups. 'Hold on! We'll have
some of those!' Serena found herself giving up the
empty cup, holding a cool, full one pressed on her by
Hilda. Well, why not? One more, then she would head
for the soft drinks. It had been too long since she went
out socially, and her head simply wasn't used to
alcohol.

'You're sailing to Mexico?' She turned her back on
Neil and his blonde, managed to sound interested in
Hilda and her Mexican odyssey. She would play the
game, make conversation, and then somehow get
herself through that mob to the door.

'That's right. Mexico for the winter, then Tahiti in the
spring. We'd like to make the San Francisco passage in
one leg, but we need one more crew member.' Hilda
grinned. 'Glen would like a man, but I'd love another
woman to talk to. How far do you want to go?'

'San Francisco,' said Serena, throwing the truth to
the winds. Why not pretend this was real, that she was
ready to set off into Adventureland? 'I'd like to crew as
far as San Francisco, just to get a little more sea
experience.' More? That was a laugh. She had never
been out of sight of land in her life.

'Super!' Hilda's voice rose to a scream, 'Glen! Hey,
Glen! Over here! This is Serena and she wants to go to
San Francisco.'

He was a heavy-set, slippery kind of man. Serena stiffened and took another sip of the cool wine as he said, 'Hi, Serena. What kind of experience do you have?' He leered and said, 'Sailing experience, that is.'

She eased away until she came up against a hard barrier of bodies. 'Not a lot.' She made her voice casual, her eyes watching him because he was the kind of man you shouldn't trust. 'I've sailed the gulf islands for years.' Well, it wasn't exactly a lie. She had been sailing five or six times in a three-year period. Glen was starting to shake his head and she found herself adding, 'And last year I crewed on a forty-footer from Juan de Fuca Strait to San Francisco.' Her lie dropped into the conversation with all the authenticity of truth. She turned away then, but Hilda's hand clutched at her arm.

'Did you?' Hilda squealed. 'Oh, lovely! We've never done it before, and we did so want to get someone experienced. Tell me, what was it like? Were you scared when you were alone on watch at night?'

'Don't be ridiculous, Hilda!' Glen's voice was harsh, and Serena found herself wishing Hilda would slap him. 'We're leaving on September the first,' he told Serena, his voice turned pleasant.

'Sorry,' she lied, 'but September is no good for me. I'm a teacher. I have to be in class the first week of September.'

'Glen and Hilda?' Her heart almost stopped when his voice spoke behind her. What was it about the man's voice? And his eyes, for that matter? They should be packaged with a warning for lonely women! She felt his smile, heard him asking Glen, 'Is your boat the *North Star*? I thought so. I ran into friends of yours in Mexico last winter. On board *Adventurer*. They said to say hello if I ever ran into you.'

'*Adventurer?*' said Glen blankly. 'I don't think——'

'Of course!' shrieked Hilda. 'Of course we remember *Adventurer!* Don't you remember, Glen?'

Serena saw the laughter in Neil's eyes and knew her suspicion was correct as he said smoothly, 'You'll be happy to hear that they had a good passage down. Right now they're waiting out the hurricane season in the Gulf of California.' His smile was brilliant. It succeeded in charming Hilda, and almost seemed to convince Glen that he should remember a boat he had never seen in his life.

'We meet so many boats,' Glen was saying.

'I know what it's like,' agreed the younger man. He turned to Serena. 'I'm sorry about the interruption a few minutes ago. Could we finish our conversation now?' He flashed a smile at Hilda and said, 'I'll bring her right back to you.'

'There's no such boat as *Adventurer!*' she accused him as he led her away. Her words hissed through the racket around them. She didn't know why she could not pull her arm away from his guiding hand. It was one thing to have her breath cut short when a stranger looked at her, quite another to let him lead her away without protest. Especially a man who told lies so easily.

'There is,' he insisted. He opened a door she hadn't realised was there.

'Where are you taking me? I don't want to——' But, somehow, she was walking where he led her, outside on to an empty veranda. Then he stopped and she did, too, suddenly aware of the hard excitement of his fingers on her arm.

'There,' he said, freeing her arm. 'Now we can talk.'

'Finish our conversation?' She met his eyes. It was a little easier out here in the shadows. He couldn't see her eyes well enough to know the effect he had on her. Or could he? She tried to remember that he was a man who told smooth lies, that she shouldn't be attracted, that she wasn't ready for this kind of thing yet, in any case. 'You told Glen and Hilda you wanted to finish our conversation. You don't always tell the truth, do you?' Her voice was rising, accusing. 'We never started a conversation. How did you know the name of their boat?'

'It was on his name-tag.' His eyelashes dropped as he focused on her lips, then down to the shapely female curves under her casually attractive dress. She endured a heart-stopping instant of silence before he murmured, 'Didn't we start a conversation? I thought we did, Serena-with-no-last-name. I had the feeling that I've known you for years.'

'Like your friend from Tahiti?' she snapped. Her fingers touched the label stuck to her bodice. She had written only 'Serena' on it, but he said her name as if he knew everything. This was definitely getting out of hand.

'An old friend,' he agreed. 'Her name's Gail.' He was obviously not embarrassed about Gail's clinging to him with such enthusiasm. He smiled and said, 'I can't help hoping you'll be an old friend, too.'

Gail had been his lover. It had been in her eyes, her voice, the way she touched him. It was frightening the way this man seemed to radiate such a raw attraction, terrifying how it seemed to work on her.

He pushed back a lock of hair that insisted on drooping over his forehead. 'You have the feel of an old friend.' His smile changed as his voice dropped. 'Perhaps more than a friend, but I think that's the best place to start.'

Sassy schoolboys had taught her to be quick with a comeback, but she could not think of a thing to say. She took refuge in changing the subject. 'What about *Adventurer*? You were lying to those people.'

'But not to you, Serena. It's a Canadian boat, sailing the Baha area.' Somehow his words sounded true. 'They really did sail south from here last year.'

'You were lying when you told them about it. I know you were.'

He stared at her for a long moment, then asked softly, 'How can you deny we're old friends? The only other person who always knows when I'm not telling the truth is Zeb.'

'Zeb? Who——'

'My older brother, the family rock.' He shifted, leaning against the railing. She had the feeling that he was ready to stand here talking to her forever as he said, 'Zeb comes to my mind because he witnessed a lot of my young indiscretions and you have the rather exciting feeling of a future indiscretion. And you're right. *Adventurer* is real enough, but her owners never mentioned Glen and Hilda to me.' She saw a flash of impishness in his face, than a sudden seriousness. 'I'm not in the habit of manufacturing stories, not since I turned ten or so. But I badly wanted to get you away from them. Another five minutes and they'd have had their leaving date changed and you signed up as crew.' He crossed his arms and she thought he looked like a judge, a cold man who could hand out harsh sentences.

'To get me away?' It seemed important to clarify this. She tossed back her curls, tried to sound as harsh as he looked, tried to believe that this was happening to Serena Jones, a twenty-nine-year-old teacher whose only adventures had been in dreams. 'Why? This is a crew party. I'm here looking for a boat, and they're looking for crew. So why——'

'Are you really?' His words snapped at her.

'Am I really what?' She shifted nervously without knowing why, hugged herself w th her arms although it was not cold.

'Looking for a boat to crew on?' He stepped closer and she felt the force of him. She would not have wanted him as an enemy. She had a strong feeling that this was the moment she should tell him the truth about why she was really here.

'I——'

'A lot of women come to these things looking for a man, not a crewing job.' His thumb caught the underside of her jaw and pressed up, urging her eyes to his.

'I'm not looking for a man.' It seemed like a lie, because when he touched her she felt like a tremulous woman waiting for her lover. She clenched her fingers on the empty paper cup and heard it crumple. 'I came—I—it's a crew party, and this is the year that I would have been going to the South Pacific if it had worked out, but——' The sad failure of Terry's dreams tumbled on her lips, but something in his eyes stopped her.

'Some men come looking for crew,' he told her harshly. 'Some are looking for a woman.' He was frowning, as if this was dead serious.

'Is that why you came?' she breathed.

'I came for crew, because mine stood me up at the last moment. But——' his fingers possessed her arms. He did not draw her closer, but she could feel the strength and knew she could not fight him 'if you are here looking for a man,' he said oddly, 'I've a feeling it had better be me.' She stumbled a little as he released her arms, then his thumb pressed hard under her chin, but she was positive that he did not know he was hurting. She shook her head and he said, 'In any case, you're my crew.'

His words echoed over the empty veranda. She had never seen him in her life until he'd stopped her heart at the entrance. This was impossible. The time was all wrong. She was only beginning to think about loving again, some day when the right man came, but never a strange, wild man like this. Someone from her own tame, secure world.

'You're crazy.' It was a whisper, not the shout it should have been. 'You don't know me, and——'

He smiled suddenly, and she felt some tension flow out of her. 'I'm not crazy. Impulsive, I admit, but I have faith in my impulses, and this one tells me that I've found the perfect crew.'

'No! I——' How had this happened? She had come as a ghost slipping through, to listen and watch and say goodbye to a dream that should have died with Terry.

He stepped back and she could breathe more easily. 'Hold on a second. I'll get us a drink.'

This would be the moment to leave, but she stood at the railing of the veranda without knowing why she stayed, staring at her crumpled cup. She had never done anything like this before in her life, never met anyone like him. Perhaps that was why she could not walk away while he was gone.

Then he was back before she had quite decided to stay, handing her yet another cup of the wine and telling her, 'You don't want to go with Hilda and Glen, I can assure you. I know the type. You'd be dodging him every mile of the way, while Hilda stays down below chained to the stove and violently sick all the way. Leave it for one of those twenty-year-old boys who want to sail so much that they'll take any amount of slavery!'

His voice was becoming impersonal, making it easier

for her to breathe, letting sanity return. For just a moment she had believed he wanted her as a woman, that he meant to have her. She knew he was attracted, but this line of his was just a joke. Or was it? What if he felt the same awareness she had experienced? For a few minutes she had felt such a strong attraction that she could even understand how a woman might become involved in a casual sexual encounter, despite all the risks.

Casual? *Nothing* about her reaction to this man was casual.

'I——' Her voice was ridiculously weak, then strengthening. 'I wouldn't have gone with them. They're leaving in September.'

'And you're teaching in September?' How long had he been listening to her conversation with Glen and Hilda? 'What do you teach, Serena?'

'Languages.' She grasped at the everyday topic. 'I teach in a high school. Mainly French. I have one German class.'

'You speak French? And German?' She nodded. He smiled, asked, 'Spanish?'

'A little. I'm working on Spanish and Italian.'

'A world traveller?' She shook her head and he said, 'How do you get all those languages? Your parents were diplomats? Travelling minstrels?'

She laughed then. 'No, my father was a vet until he retired. My mom was an organiser—she organised my dad's life. They've never been anywhere but Canada and the States. I haven't, either. I just like languages, and I seem to have an aptitude for them.'

'So you teach. Do you like teaching? What age?'

Did he really want to hear all this? 'Fourteen to sixteen-year-olds. Yes, I like it, though sometimes I——' She caught herself on the verge of telling him she yearned for a real adventure in her life.

'Sometimes you'd like a change? Like last year, sailing to San Francisco?' So he had heard her lies to Glen and Hilda. She nodded mutely, hypnotised by his low voice. 'Is that why you're here, to do it again?'

'Yes.' Why was she lying to him? Why did it seem so impossible to tell him it was all a crazy impulse, that she did not belong in this place with these people?

'I'm leaving in four days. I'll be in San Francisco well before the end of August.' His eyes held hers. This sounded like an invitation and she did not know what to say. 'Will you come?'

'I——' She was spinning, had a crazy fear that this man would sweep her away, his will conquering hers without those dark eyes even showing sign of strain. 'That's too soon. There would be too much to get ready.'

'Not much. You'd only need your toothbrush and so forth. Something to read on the daytime watches, though I've got quite a stock of reading material aboard. Bring warm clothes.' He sounded very matter of fact suddenly. 'It's colder than you will expect——No, you've done it before, haven't you? You'll know. *Passagemaker's* equipped, already provisioned for a crew of two. My son was going to be with me, but last week—well, he can't make it.' She saw a flash of uncertainty on his face, then he said, 'He'll join me in San Francisco.'

He had a son. That meant a marriage, a wife. She was not a nosy woman. She would not have asked, but he seemed to take the question from her mind. 'No,' he said. 'Sandra—my wife died five years ago. She was hit at a crossroads by a speeding car.'

'I didn't—I——' Her eyes fell to the label on her dress. Sandra . . . Serena. She whispered, 'The names aren't that different.'

He said quietly, 'Perhaps not, but the women are very different. And, no, Serena, I am not trying to raise ghosts from the past.'

She swallowed. Perhaps *he* wasn't, but her ghosts were alive and strong. Tonight was not supposed to be real, but Terry's sailing dream seemed to have a lot of power for her right now.

Neil said, 'We're talking about crews.' His smile grew again, but she could not answer it. His fingers brushed her hand, so briefly that there was no threat. 'And friendship, I think.' Then his eyes flashed something more for a moment. 'The rest is up to fate, isn't it?'

Fate. Did she believe in fate? She should. Terry dreaming, then his dreams so cruelly destroyed. 'Tell me about your passage,' he urged her, and she blinked, bewildered.

'What passage?'

'Last year. You sailed to San Francisco.'

'Oh!' She swallowed. How could she tell him that she had lied, that there had been no passage except the one she and Terry had planned to make? 'I don't—I— what do you want to know?'

He shrugged. 'How long? What kind of winds did you have?'

'We didn't . . .'

'You didn't have any winds?' He frowned. 'That's miserable, when there's no wind out there. With a brisk northerly it can be a great downhill run, but——'

'No, I meant——' She would never see him again. She would remember him, though, and she wanted him to remember her without frowning. 'It wasn't a spectacular passage.'

She smiled, because his laughter was low and catching. 'Serena, they're all interesting. You said you did it in one leg to San Francisco. How long?'

'Eight days.' He was going to insist on the details. She had read so many articles and stories to Terry that the lies seemed to come like truth. 'We left from Victoria and sailed out Juan de Fuca Strait, then stayed about a hundred miles offshore until we headed in for San Francisco.'

'What kind of winds?' He was intent, listening as much to the tone of her voice and the expression in her shadowed eyes as to her words.

'For the first couple of days we had about twenty knots from the north-west.' She knew north-west was the usual direction in that area in summer. 'Then it picked up to gale force.' She couldn't help grinning. She had said that as if she were a seasoned sailor, speaking of gales as casually as traffic jams. She added quickly, 'The gale blew itself out after about twenty-four hours,' because she couldn't manufacture a disaster at sea. She hadn't read enough stories for that.

He was frowning as he calculated mentally. 'You must have had light winds the rest of the way, or you'd have made it in less than eight days. After all, you had twenty knots and more driving you the first few hundred miles.'

'Yes,' she agreed, trapped deeper in the lie. The trip had been only a plan—Terry's dream, which should have been given up years ago.

'What kind of rig? What design boat? What was her name?' His questions were smothering her. 'I might know it. If the boat got to Mexico, I probably saw it down there.' He seemed certain of that and she felt panic growing. How many lies before she could leave? How on earth had she got into this?

'I don't think they got to Mexico,' she improvised wildly, her restless fingers making unruly curls even wilder. 'They were going to Hawaii from San Francisco. It was a forty-foot cutter. I——' What name? What was a name for a boat? A name he had never heard of? She changed the subject desperately. 'How big is your boat? Were you in Mexico last year?'

'Forty-three feet. And she's a cutter. You'll be right at home on her.' His eyes were intent. At any moment he would uncover her lies. It was going to be horribly embarrassing, trying to explain.

'I don't think—actually, I wasn't able to do all the sail handling.' That was reasonable, she thought. She was only a couple of inches over five feet, and forty-foot boats had big lines to haul on. 'I needed help working the sails. You need someone stronger to——'

'That's no problem.' His muscles rippled under his T-shirt as he said, '*Passagemaker* is well-rigged. I have big winches to handle the sails. On short passages I can single-hand her, but offshore it's a matter of safety to have more crew to keep a watch at night. Offshore I make a practice of having two people topsides when sails need tending—one in the cockpit and one on deck working sail.'

'I don't think I'm what you want. On the trip I did—I'm not—— You should get one of those young fellows, strong and——'

'I don't need a muscle man, just someone to share the watches.' Of course. She would be the one in the cockpit while he did the man's work. She laughed at his assumption that the women belonged in the cockpit, and his laughter answered hers. 'Listen, I won't work you to death. Just seven days at sea, maybe ten, and you and I can handle it with no problem. Lots of couples make the passage without additional crew, just one man and one woman.'

'But——' For the first time, she actually considered

doing it. It had been Terry's dream, but she had caught the excitement. And he was right. There was time. She had no commitments, a lonely August stretched ahead. Everyone she knew was either working or away on holidays. Her parents were on an extended trip to the Maritime Provinces.

'Friday,' he said, his voice carrying the tones of a man accustomed to persuading others to his way. 'Tomorrow you could come down to see the boat, if you like. I'll be out of town Wednesday and Thursday. You could move your stuff aboard Thursday night and get a good sleep before we set sail Friday.'

She shook her head. 'You can't—you can't just talk to me for five minutes and—— Do you always decide things so impulsively? Maybe I'll get out there and freak out on you. Maybe——'

'You did it last summer. It's not as if you're inexperienced.' She saw the lines radiate out from the corner of his eyes as he frowned. 'If you don't want to crew, you wouldn't be here tonight.' There was nothing she could say. Only more lies. There had already been too many. Every time she opened her mouth she seemed to get deeper. He said, 'I assure you I'm a competent seaman, if that's what's making you hesitate.'

She shook her head mutely, felt her curls tumbling everywhere. 'No, I just——'

'Who was with you?' His voice had gentled, as if he felt the sadness of her memories although he did not understand them. 'How many on board?'

Another lie, and she went deeper. 'The owner of the boat. He was going to single-hand it after San Francisco, but he wanted crew for the first part, the long passage.' No, that was wrong. She had said Hawaii, and San Francisco to Hawaii was a far longer passage than that first leg. She spoke quickly, covering her mistake. 'He—ah, he didn't mind single-handing on the open ocean, but along the coast he was afraid of the shipping lanes.'

'I don't wonder. He wouldn't be the first boat to run into a freighter while the captain slept. If you're concerned about that, you and I will be going far offshore, well out of the shipping lanes. Two can keep a good watch out there. Who else was on board? You and the captain and——?'

'Terry.' She swallowed, said, 'My husband.'

'Your husband?' It was a question, but she only stared at him until he asked, 'Where is he now?'

'He died. Last year.'

He did not move, but she felt him giving her more space, as if her words had created a barrier. 'I'm sorry, Serena.'

When the silence grew too full, she licked her lips and managed, 'I think I'd better go. I really didn't—I sort of got to this party by accident. I——His gentle fingers on her arm drained the words away. She looked up at him, imagining she could see the deepness of his dark eyes even out here without lights.

'Serena, I'm—I'm not going to lie to you.' His voice was even deeper than she remembered. 'I'm sorry for your loss. I hate to think of you hurt. But I'm glad you're free. It would be a hell of a shock to me to find out that you belonged to someone else.'

'You . . .' This was not the kind of event that happened in Serena Jones' rather uneventful life, and she knew nothing about this man, except that he had a boat, was heading for Mexico and needed crew to San Francisco. 'You're crazy. You—listen, I'm going. I've got to get out of here. I don't——'

'I'll take you home.'

'No, I—really. Tonight is—I'm sorry, but it's . . . Terry died a year ago. August the first. I can't—I . . .'

His fingers held her forearm as he stared down at her. 'He died at sea?'

'No. No!' She simply *had* to get out of here. 'Please!'

He made her give him her telephone number before she left. Then she was gone and he realised that she might have deliberately given him a wrong number. He hurried outside to where he had seen a pay telephone, and spent a frustrating ten minutes waiting for a dippy-looking woman to terminate an endless and senseless conversation.

He found himself wondering why it mattered so much that he had the right number.

Damn! How did you find a woman named Serena in a city this size? She taught at high school. How many high schools were there in Victoria? Private school or public? Could you find out about school employees in the middle of summer holidays? Why had he come on so bloody strong, anyway? It wasn't his style. Face it, he had been alone too long. The last couple of years he had been working too hard to spend much time pursuing any of the women who stirred his interest.

He had never felt quite like this before. She had looked at him with brown, vulnerable eyes, and he had known he must somehow prevent her from walking into his life and right back out before he could find out why his heart thundered so wildly just looking at her eyes. He felt ashamed of his relief when she told him her husband was dead.

But a year was long enough for the worst to be over, although the memories would come back to her in odd moments, the sense of loss and loneliness. He knew about that only too well.

He had come to this party to try to find someone to replace Keith as crew, but from the moment he'd seen her he'd had only one objective. Serena. All right, he'd decided, so he would kill two birds with one stone. She would be his crew. There would be the cruise to San Francisco, then, when they were quietly at anchor, a few days before they went their separate ways. Cool, practical Zeb would never understand, but if this woman slipped out of his life tonight he was going to regret it. Neil suspected that Zeb had never had a wild, unplanned relationship in his entire life.

Finally, the idiot woman on the telephone was done. Neil fumbled for a quarter and, slipped it into the slot, only to have it rejected. What was he doing, anyway? Hoping there would be no answer, because she could not possibly be home yet. Damn machine! Didn't it know that American money was worth more on the international market than Canadian?

'Hey!' The girl behind the counter was deep in conversation with a young, handsome man. 'Does either of you have a quarter?' He felt an uncharacteristic embarrassment when he realised that the girl thought he was panhandling. He held up his coin. 'This American quarter won't work.'

Back at the telephone, the machine accepted the new coin. This was futile, because she had been running and the number would not be hers. His fears were confirmed when the ringing stopped and a woman's voice, light and eager, said, 'Hi! Is that you, honey?'

'Sorry, it isn't.' He might as well ask. 'Is Serena in?'

'Oh!' The voice was startled, slightly embarrassed. 'I thought you were my boyfriend. He was supposed to call and——No, I'm sorry. Serena won't be in till later. Can I say who called?'

He hadn't lost her, after all.

His brother Zeb would have cautioned that he had not yet persuaded the lady to crew for him, but he did not even consider that he might fail. If she meant to say no, why would she give him her telephone number?

CHAPTER TWO

IT SEEMED as if the strong tides of the North Pacific were sweeping her out to sea. Either that, or the man, because Neil Turner was not taking no for an answer.

He called early in the morning after the party. She was in the kitchen, drinking coffee with Diane before her flatmate went to work. Her comfortable housecoat was a contrast to Diane's grey suit. Diane was always tidier, smoother, her hair perfectly restrained where Serena's was wild. It was Diane, quicker and more efficient, who answered the ringing telephone.

'It's him. The man from last night.' She held it out, grinning at Serena's nervousness.

'Neil here,' he identified himself as soon as she answered the telephone. 'What's your last name?'

She had dreamed about the man, had woken telling herself he had nothing but a telephone number, and she would give him no more. Last night was history, put to rest with the dreams she had shared with Terry. But if Neil Turner was history he did not know it, and she found her lips telling him, 'Jones.'

'I'll pick you up in an hour.'

'What? Why?' She still had her coffee-cup in her hand, but her fingers were trembling and there was a wet splotch of coffee on the pale blue of her sleeve. This was ridiculous. She had told a pack of lies last night, and the only solution was to turn her back on him and never see him again.

'You're coming to see my boat. Remember? Wear

slacks and soft shoes.'

She laughed. Typical sailor, thinking of his boat first. 'No heel marks on your teak decks?'

'That's right. What's your address?' And she told him, despite the cautious voice echoing in her mind. 'What am I getting into?' she wailed as she sank back down at their re-varnished garage-sale kitchen table. 'He wants me to sail to San Francisco with him!'

'Why not?' Diane brushed a crumb of toast away from her immaculate jacket. 'You've got nothing to do until school starts, and you love sailing.'

'Georgia Strait and the Gulf Islands.' Diane had no idea at all. What could she know about the ocean when she spent her life telling other people's hair what to do? 'That's not the same thing as the open ocean, for pete's sake!' Diane shrugged that away with the ignorance of a landlubber, and Serena went on, 'He's a stranger. You want me to go off in a little boat with a man I don't know from Adam? He might be a monster!'

'Is he? I thought he sounded like a real hunk.'

Serena laughed. 'Yes—no. You'd like him. He's not exactly conventional, but——' Impulsive. He'd admitted to that. But good at reading people, although not good enough to know she was lying. And strong. Friends, he had said, and maybe more. He would be here in an hour—less—and there weren't enough good friends in the world to plan on throwing one away.

Or a lover? If she let him lead her on to his boat, it might end anywhere. Her parents certainly wouldn't approve, but then they were four thousand miles away.

Terry was gone forever.

Diane pushed back her cup. 'I have to go to work, two perms first thing. Smarten up, Serena! Don't you dare pass this up! What do you think he's going to do? Take advantage of you at sea? If one or the other of you has to be awake all the way to San Francisco, you'll be too busy sleeping to get involved in an affair—unless *you* decide to really make a set for him.'

There was only one real reason for not going. Serena stared into her black coffee. 'I lied to him. I told him I'd done this before.'

'So come clean.'

Serena remembered Neil's eyes and she wasn't sure it could be that simple. 'He might change his mind if he knows I've never been to sea.'

'For heaven's sake, Serena, how often do you think you'll get a chance like this?' Never. Never again. She owed it to Terry, didn't she, to try to make at least a bit of his dream come true?

By insanity or fate, somehow she was swept through the morning. *Passagemaker* was a beautiful cutter with teak decks and varnished wooden mast. Her quarters aboard—if she came—were a secluded cabin up forward, beautiful and bright.

'I'm in the back, with the electronic equipment,' he told her, but his eyes left no doubt that if she wanted to share it his berth was wide enough for two. Yet she knew that there would be no real pressure. She could use the forward cabin and no questions would be asked.

A quick rundown on equipment and Neil's rules. He was a careful sailor, an attractive blend of adventure and caution. He gave her a list of the supplies she should bring, then he bought her fish and chips from a stand on the wharf, the food wrapped in newspaper and smelling delicious.

She had not been herself last night. Perhaps she was still not back to normal, because she found herself standing beside his rented car outside her apartment in the middle of the afternoon, listening to him say, 'All right. I'm flying to San Diego tomorrow, but I'll be back the next night. I'll see you Thursday night at the boat.'

She could not manage to tell him no, but she was *not* going. Although—damn it, it really would be exciting. She could go back to school and tell the kids she had spent August sailing to San Francisco. She grinned at that, even thought it was impossible.

It was the kind of thing you did when you were college age: taking off with a stranger, seeing the world without stopping to consider the consequences. She had never done it herself, but she had friends who had hitch-hiked across Europe, gone camping in Africa. Years ago. She would be thirty next year, far too old for ill-advised wild impulses.

He was so persuasive. It seemed impossible to use the word 'no' to Neil Turner, but if she had any sense at all she would leave town for a few days—until *Passagemaker* was gone.

On Wednesday morning she told Diane she was leaving town, going to Vancouver for a week's shopping. 'You're crazy,' said Diane, then she shrugged and left for work.

Serena called the ferry terminal for the times of the Vancouver ferry, then went into the store-room and dug out her warmest sweaters. It didn't mean anything. Just that autumn was coming, and it was easier to take the time to find winter clothes before school started.

She didn't take the ferry.

On Thursday morning she did laundry, and found herself sorting clothes as she folded them. The jeans and a couple of jogging suits in one pile. The suits

were warm and comfortable, good sailing gear. Heavy
sweater. A woollen cap in case he really meant *cold*.
Six to eight days, probably, perhaps ten or eleven if
winds were light. All those days and nights alone on a
forty-three-foot boat with Neil Turner.

Brassieres. Changes of underwear.

In the end the pile was too big to fit into her small
pack, so she borrowed Diane's soft suitcase, hoping it
would stow easily on board.

A passage at sea. The real thing. Wind and waves
and adventure. She was going. *She really was going.* As
for the lies—if he asked many more questions about
her mythical trip to San Francisco, she would take
Diane's advice and come clean, but she was going to
go sailing!

She had never been to San Francisco, not even by air
or by car. She had been across the border from
Vancouver to Blaine, but that was all. It was time,
wasn't it? Neil was paying her air fare home. He said
he always did that for people he asked to crew. She
would be left with enough money in the bank to spend
a week at a modest hotel in San Francisco. It would be
a super holiday!

She fully expected a telephone call from her mother,
or perhaps Terry's ghost. Terry was supposed to have
been the one going sailing with her. But no one called,
no one tried to stop her. She wasn't sure if that was
good or bad but, whichever, she didn't seem to want
to stop herself.

Diane drove her down to the docks on Thursday
evening, locked her car and came along for a look at
the darkened boat. Neil wasn't there. He had said he
might not arrive until late, and had given her the
combination to his lock. When she dialled the
numbers, the door to the companionway swung open.

It took a minute to find the light switch.

'Gorgeous!' breathed Diane, looking at the way the varnished wood shone, at the galley with gas range and microwave. 'No dishwasher,' she commented, and Serena laughed to cover her scared excitement.

Then she was alone, and still he had not come. He was flying into Vancouver airport, taking a late ferry across to Victoria. She took her case to her cabin but she didn't unpack it, just stowed it on the far side of the cabin. This was where she would sleep, although he had said that at sea she might want to use the pilot berth in the salon. It was more comfortable under sail.

She would use the cabin. A door was a good idea if they were to spend the next week or so together. She would sleep up front, and he would be in the back, sleeping on the berth in the navigation-room.

She shivered and wondered if she was quite sane. When she was on watch in the night she would see him sleeping every time she went into the navigation-room. It was an incredible intimacy, alone together on the ocean. Six days . . . or seven . . . or eight. Perhaps longer. She had never spent that many days in Terry's exclusive company. There had always been the rest of the world, other people around, outside. But this would be just water, and Neil.

If she picked up her bag and left quickly he would never know she had been here. She stood, tense, getting ready to run, until somehow the urge to flee faded away to nothing.

Should she go to bed? To sleep? It was late enough, but he would come back. He would open the door and climb down the stairs to the companionway. Then forward, and she would be there, sleeping. She would rather he came and found her with her clothes on, her feet on the floor.

She tried to find a book that would interest her, keep her eyes off the clock. He had told her there was lots to read, but most of them were sailing books. He didn't do a lot of light reading. There were some heavy-duty novels, the kind she would only attack if she knew she had a lot of time and mental energy to devote to reading. She wished now that she had brought some of her own books. It was an evening for a light romance, or for a mystery.

Why didn't he come? She prowled, waiting, ending up in the navigation-room looking at the instruments, wishing she knew something about Loran and Satnav and radar. This boat was filled with equipment she had never seen before.

There were more books here, mostly chart books and reference books. A French dictionary. A Spanish dictionary. Well, she could talk French with him if he wanted, but her Spanish was skimpy. Charts in the drawers. Was she snooping? Maybe, but none of these things seemed personal.

She picked up a thick, leather-bound book embossed with the boat's name. She took it out carefully and it fell open to a page half filled with dark, masculine handwriting. Once, she had made a hobby of analysing handwriting and now she traced the strong lines with her finger, telling herself that the man was here. Impulsive and strong. He liked to dominate his environment, but he was sensitive, too, and somewhere in the curve of his capitals she thought she detected tinges of loneliness, although the purposeful quickness of his writing almost concealed it.

She sat down, then jerked back to her feet. He would be back soon. She did not want him to find her curled up on his bed, and this was the place he slept.

She took the book forward and propped a cushion behind her to make the salon settee more comfortable.

Passagemaker's history was all here, and perhaps much of Neil's as well. The last entry was made a week ago, his arrival in Victoria, a day passage from Seattle. Why had he crossed north to Canada prior to starting this trip? There was no answer in the details of the passage.

She turned back. The book was thick, all the way back to the day *Passagemaker* was launched, eight years ago. The first entries were in a variety of hands, so Neil had not been the only one to sail this boat. Another masculine hand had filled in the details in the front of the log, the writing strong and regular but without Neil's impulsive strokes. Were all sailors strong, practical men? If so, Terry could never have been one of them. He had been too much a dreamer, too little a strong man.

She read the words on the first page: 'Designer, Zeb Turner. Builder, Turner Enterprises, San Diego.'

Zeb. 'My big brother. The family rock.' The man with the steady handwriting. Designer, perhaps, but big brother Zeb had not sailed this boat very often. The first pages were varied. Zeb's name appeared, and Neil's. She found one entry with Sandra's name. Neil's wife. She read the bare details of a seven-day cruise, San Diego to the Channel Islands. Neil had made most of the entries, there were only one or two in Sandra's feminine hand. Sandra. What did her handwriting reveal? A woman who preferred stability to adventure, who would hold her family close, too close. Or perhaps that was fancy, guesswork, because Sandra's name did not appear again, and Neil's seldom.

His wife had not taken to sailing.

The pages that followed could only mean that the boat had been chartered for a couple of years. A variety of captains wrote in the log, destinations all along the west coast from Alaska to Mexico. Neither Zeb nor Neil seemed to have taken much pleasure from this beautiful vessel in her first years.

Then Neil's handwriting leaped off the page. 'Began provisioning for offshore passage.' The date was September, four years ago. 'Sandra—my wife died five years ago.' A year of mourning? Then reaching out for a new life, trying to forget the loss? The pages that followed detailed an intensive series of jobs to prepare *Passagemaker* for sea. Engine overhaul. Changes in the navigation station. Provisioning. Keeping busy, she thought, trying not to feel the loneliness, the emptiness.

He had left in November, he and his son Keith alone on board. She turned ahead, found where he arrived in Tahiti. This had not looked like a private diary, but she could not help feeling that she was probing where she had no right.

The blonde at the party had not seen him since Tahiti, and she had flowed into his arms like a lover. There she was, a name written in the account of a day sail. Gail. The only woman's name in all those months of sailing, all the years since that one week when Sandra had been aboard.

A note in the log marked Keith's flying home to San Diego to visit his uncle for two weeks. Gail's name was in the log during those fourteen days, then it disappeared and *Passagemaker* set sail for Australia.

Two weeks. She swallowed, hoping it had helped, that when he left for Australia he was not still aching for the woman who died.

Serena fell asleep somewhere in the monotonous

details of Neil's crossing of the Atlantic a year later. Day after day of nothing but wind directions and speeds, calculations of longitude and latitude. An empty ocean, an apparently uneventful passage.

When the weight of the book left her hands she woke with abrupt panic. It was dark, but faint light through the portholes showed the strangely familiar silhouette and her fear left her.

She struggled to sit up. He touched her shoulder lightly, saying, 'Don't get up. Sleep there if you're comfortable.' Soft, fluffy warmth floated over her. His hands hardly touched as they tucked the sleeping-bag around her. 'Have a good sleep. You'll need your rest.' He sounded sleepy, too, as if he had travelled too far, too quickly.

'What did you do after the Atlantic?' she asked, her fingers curling where the book had been, closing on empty air. 'Did you go back to San Diego?'

'Mexico.' He stepped back, the dark silhouette receding. 'I've been there ever since.'

Doing what? she wondered. He was not a man to sit idle for three years. 'You're not in Mexico now.'

'No,' he agreed, a tired smile in his voice. 'I'm here, taking the boat back. Go to sleep.'

But how had it got here if he had been in Mexico?

'Tomorrow,' he said, seeming again to read her mind. 'Ask tomorrow. I'm too tired to talk tonight.' He reached over her and a curtain fell across the porthole. 'Goodnight, Serena. Sleep——' he chuckled and finished '—serenely.' Then he left her alone, disappearing into the back of the boat, to his cabin, the place he shared with a roomful of instruments.

She picked up the sleeping-bag and padded forward in her bare feet. Had he taken her shoes off? She closed the door and lay on a strange berth, not expecting to sleep at all but losing consciousness almost as soon as her head touched the pillow.

She woke the instant his knuckles rapped on her closed door. 'Morning, Serena. Your breakfast is on the table. When you've had it, I could use some help up top.' Brisk, businesslike.

He was gone by the time she had hurried into her clothes and opened the door. She could hear footsteps overhead, back and forth, things moving, little bangs and creaks that were boat sounds she had not heard in years, not since the days when she and Terry had actually gone sailing.

She hadn't realised how hungry she was until she smelled the crisp bacon smell, then she remembered that she'd skipped supper the night before. Had he expected her to be up earlier, cooking breakfast?

The bacon was gone and she had eaten half of the egg when the engine started. At first she thought it was another boat nearby, then she felt the vibration all through her. Surely he was not leaving yet? There had to be time, a slow leaving, giving her a chance to . . .

She dashed up the stairs, emerged into the cockpit and could not see him at all. Then he was there, standing on the wharf, untying the spring lines and tossing them on to the deck.

Panicked, she squeaked, 'You're—we're not leaving, are we?' The second spring line hit the deck and he moved to the aft line. If he untied that one, there would be only the forward line between *Passagemaker* and the deep sea. 'What about the weather? Shouldn't we——'

He released the aft line, looped it over a docking cleat and held the coiled end towards her. 'Here, take this and stand ready to cast off when I tell you.'

No! It was one thing to sleep in his berth at the dock, but quite another to actually cast off and go out into the ocean with only this boat and the man between her and the savage sea!

'No, I—Neil, I—I've changed my mind!'

His eyes narrowed, taking in her unruly hair, her still-sleepy eyes. 'Take it easy,' he said softly. 'It'll be fine. I really do know how to sail this thing, you know.'

'But——'

He stepped closer and the rope was in her hands, her fingers clenching the white and red braided strands. His voice was careful, as if giving instructions to a child. 'Hold it in tight, then just swing it over the cleat when I say.' He walked away and the forward line came flying on to the deck in a lazy, snaking stream. She gulped as she heard it hit. Then he leaned out and caught one of the shrouds with one hand and seemed to push the forward part of the boat off as he stepped on. Then, swiftly, he was in the cockpit, pushing a lever to change the sound of that engine as his eyes swept the route he would take to clear the wharfs.

'Now, Serena, bring the aft line in.'

She twitched it and watched it slip free, then her hands were pulling in the line as the wharf slid away. Her heart pounded through every cell of her body, and she fought an insane urge to make a desperate leap for shore.

'Coil the lines and put them on top of the after cabin. I'll show you where they go once we're clear.'

He wasn't looking at her as he gave the instructions, his eyes just glanced over her as he checked for boats behind. The wheel spun and they were pulling free into the channel; the man was a stranger, his mouth frowning, his shoulders broad and muscular. She walked forward on the deck, needing to get away from him, stumbling a little because her mind was screaming at him to stop this, to turn around and let her off.

'Oh, and Serena——' His voice followed her as she walked, loud enough to overcome the sounds of engine and fresh wind.

She stopped. She had to tell him soon, beg him to turn back, because this was a mistake, a horrible mistake.

'Bring in the fenders, would you? They go in those holders on the aft rail!'

The lines. The fenders. They were for docking, and he had no plans for docking for at least a week now. They would leave the land far behind. She could imagine being away from land, only grey ocean and angry clouds, and she should have known it would be a barren terror she could not survive.

She turned and stared back at him, and he was the monster Diane had laughed about, although he looked more like a man from the cover of a book: confident at the helm of his boat, his hair wind-lashed, his dark glasses shielding the sun and hiding him from her.

'Beautiful, isn't it?'

She looked forward again, her eyes going where his did, but she could not see the beauty. The wind was coming up. By this afternoon Juan de Fuca Strait would be wild and white. That was only the beginning. She thought she could survive a wild sail in the Strait if nightfall meant she would be back on dry land. But she would be at sea, where the waves got bigger and bigger and there was no place to run.

She walked back to him. Why hadn't she thought of all this yesterday, or the day before? Why had the words 'out at sea' slipped past her mind without her knowing they meant terror? How could he smile when the ocean was so horribly wide and terrible?

'Neil, I—you know, I haven't been sailing for a long time. I——'

'Don't worry.' She was so close that she could almost make out his eyes through the dark glasses. 'I know, Serena. Over a year. It's all right. Give yourself a little time. I'm not going to expect too much of you until you've got your sea-legs again.'

Sea-legs? She had *never* developed sea legs. Inland water legs at best. How was she going to persuade him to turn back? It seemed impossible. It was in his face, in the steady sureness of *Passagemaker* ploughing through the waves. The voyage had begun. There was no turning back. She was going to have an adventure, but she knew now that she did not want an adventure! In a book, sure, but not this frightening reality.

There was no way around it: she was sailing to San Francisco with a man she had known for only four days.

He knew something was wrong. She was too tense. At least once she had tried to ask him to turn back. Maybe she was remembering other trips, another man, or perhaps she was nervous after a year on land. Whatever, it seemed a good idea to pass over it lightly, give her time to get over her wariness. He decided not to put up sail yet, to avoid the tiring beat to windward as they fought their way out Juan de Fuca Strait.

He showed her where to stow the lines, told her to relax. 'We'll just be running on the motor until we clear Cape Flattery.' He thought she seemed relieved, but surprised. He explained, 'There's no point exhausting ourselves at the beginning of the journey.'

He gave her the wheel after he'd cleared Victoria

harbour, deliberately not turning on the autopilot while he watched her handle the boat. He had never expected Serena to help hauling on lines or setting sail, but if she couldn't keep a watch and steer the boat he would have been in trouble. It was all right, though. She steered a reasonable compass course and he gave her a while to get the feel of it, then he turned on the autopilot.

Then things started getting worse, quickly. She knew nothing at all about any of the instruments. He couldn't believe that she could have been to sea and be so ignorant of modern marine electronics.

'Hardly anybody sets to sea without either Loran or Satnav these days.' What kind of boat had she crewed on, anyway? He saw her face close him out. Memories again? 'There's no time for memories now,' he told her impatiently. 'We've got a passage to make. We'll forget the Satnav for the time being, but you'd better learn a bit about the radar and the Loran. You can't take a watch if you don't know where the hell the boat is and what's out there!'

'Don't shout at me!' She pushed her hair back and he watched the curls tumble and tried to tell himself she would learn soon enough, that those eyes were intelligent. He forced his temper down and started explaining, but he wondered if he would get any sleep at all until they were out of the shipping channels.

He could usually trust his instincts, but this time his hormones had overwhelmed his brains. He should have asked her a lot of questions before taking her on as crew, instead of railroading her into it because he wanted her in his bed.

He made her go down to her cabin to sleep in the afternoon, then he turned over the watch to her at six in the evening and hoped nothing would go wrong.

He knew it wasn't going to work, although he thought he might catch perhaps thirty minutes' sleep before she called him for help.

Then he went to bed, but when dark came he had to get up and check that she had turned on the navigation lights. She hadn't, although she had thought to turn the radar on. He went back to bed, but he didn't sleep.

He took the watch at ten, snapping at her and not even wanting to apologise. He was too tired. Damn it! Maybe he should put it at Neah Bay and drop her off there. He'd be better single-handing than worrying about his crew.

No, Neah Bay was out of the question. After entering Canada he couldn't put his anchor down in the US again without clearing Customs, and there was no longer any damned Customs station at Neah Bay! He'd have to go all the way back to Port Angeles. It would be simpler to go back to Victoria and dump her on her doorstep. Then, if he wanted to pursue the woman, as a woman, he could do it on land some other time. After all, there were jets, and he wasn't that firmly tied in Mexico that he couldn't make a trip north again.

The wind had stiffened as evening deepened. *Passagemaker* was making slow progress under engine power. If he turned and set sail, he'd be back in Victoria by the next evening, but the thought of going without sleep for that long wasn't particularly inviting.

He went down and checked his position on the Loran, plotted it on the chart and decided that he could make a decent course under sail and manage to clear Cape Flattery quicker than he could under engine alone. He went forward to the gallery, poured himself a cup of coffee and checked that everything was well

stowed for sailing because they were going to heel
hard when he got the sails up.

The door to the forward cabin was closed. It was a
damned good thing the autopilot was capable of
handling the helm, because if he called down for help
she would never hear him through that closed door
with the sounds of the water on the hull and the wind
in the rigging.

To hell with her! Let her sleep. He took his coffee
into the cockpit and placed it in a gimballed holder,
then checked everything again, put on his safety
harness, and went forward to raise the main. For once,
he thought that Zeb had a point—decisions should be
made slowly, considered. Impulsiveness was for
youngsters.

He stopped his fuming before he started working.
There were enough risks to working sails in a twenty-
knot wind that he wasn't about to do it in a temper.
He concentrated on the sailing, tried to forget about
the woman sleeping below. He put a reef in the main
before he raised it. There was too much wind for full
sail. Once the sail was up, the autopilot set off course,
so he killed the engine and made a rough adjustment
to the course, then went forward to raise the stays'l for
better balance.

He started feeling happier the instant the engine
sound died. He hated the noise, although he would
never set to sea without a good engine. But this was
better, far better. They heeled over about twenty
degrees to port and ploughed through the water at
seven knots, wind and water and *Passagemaker* all
working together. It was great sailing, the moon high-
lighting the mountains and glistening on the white
sails, the stars sparkling overhead. It was a beautiful
wind! When he got Tatoosh Lighthouse on his beam,

he'd turn to run with the wind and put up more sail, then sweep out clear of the shipping lanes.

San Francisco, here we come, flying all the way! As for Serena Jones, let her sleep from here to kingdom come if she wanted. He laughed when a wave hit the rub rail and shot clear into the cockpit, but he decided he'd better change. He couldn't afford to get cold and wet with the long night-watch ahead.

He checked the radar first. There was a big green blip that he'd been watching for an hour. A freighter, but it was going to clear them easily. A smaller blip was a good five miles away, nothing to worry about yet. He would be happier once he was out of the shipping lanes.

He hadn't realised that Serena was up until he went down for his cruiser suit. Then he saw the door to the head closed, and he could hear the unmistakable sounds of her being sick. He was pulling on his cruiser suit when she came out. She looked terrible: pale and lifeless and drained of everything.

'Why didn't you tell me you'd get seasick? Have you taken anything for it?' He didn't realised how angry he sounded until he saw the hurt in her eyes. Damn it! But how the hell was he to know she needed baby-sitting? She had seemed such an independent woman, and she'd been to sea before. She stumbled past him and collapsed on to the raised floor under the dinette table, sitting there as if it were a seat, her head pushed up against the underside of the table.

He sat down beside her. 'I feel terrible,' she whispered, then her head dropped on to the upholstered seat and he knew she wasn't going to do a damned thing for herself.

He went back outside and checked that everything was under control, then he got out the first-aid kit

and found the seasickness patches. He knelt beside
her, crouching awkwardly under the table in his bulky
cruiser suit. He pushed the curls away from her ear so
he could apply the sticky round patch to the soft skin
behind her ear. She groaned when he touched her,
then her fingers fumbled for the patch he had stuck to
the soft flesh behind her earlobe.

'Don't touch it!' Her hand jerked away and he
softened his voice. 'If you get it on your hands, you've
got to wash it off right away or it'll irritate hell out of
your eyes.'

'What is it?' she managed.

Didn't she know anything? Sailors had been using
the patches for a few years now, and surely everyone
on the water knew about it? 'It's a seasickness drug.
It's absorbed through your skin slowly from that
patch. It'll last about three days, but it's going to take
twelve hours or so to become fully effective.'

He didn't know if she heard him. She pushed his
hands away and stumbled to her feet and into the
head. 'You'll feel better if you come outside,' he called
after her, then he shrugged and left her alone with her
misery.

He might as well act as if he were alone, single-
handing. He got out the little timer and hung it in its
spot in the cockpit. Later, when he was out of the
shipping lanes and on a gentler course, he would set it
and catch a few short naps. It was going to be a long
night.

At least big brother Zeb would never know about
the foolishness of this mistake. He was unlikely to
even meet the tense and nauseated Serena. By the
time they reached San Francisco, Neil was pretty sure
that his attraction to the woman would have worn off
with a vengeance.

CHAPTER THREE

SERENA had never felt more terrible in all her life. She
was probably going to die. She wished she would, or
that some merciful god would hold the world still for
her.

She had been sleeping lightly, tense because she
knew she had only a couple of hours before he woke
her, nervous of being alone on watch in the dark
hours, not knowing enough about what she was
doing. It was worse than she had feared. She hadn't
thought about the electronic equipment a seagoing
vessel carried, knew nothing about it. She had *never*
sailed at night before.

Earlier, after he had sent her down to sleep, she
had kept waking, turning on the light and checking
her watch. Not yet. She should sleep, must sleep.
Then, somehow, she was sleeping deeply, then torn
rudely awake by the sounds. The heavy snap of
Dacron sails flapping, the shudder as *Passagemaker*
hesitated, then took the wind abruptly. Then they
were heeled hard, smashing into the waves with the
bow, and she was on the wrong side of the berth,
high and falling out because the lee rails weren't up.

As she sat up, the bow went down through the sea
with a crash, jerking her stomach almost loose from
its moorings. Then again . . . and again. She curled
up on the other side, whimpering, her insides hurting horribly, but it would not stop and she finally
went lurching through the boat, stumbling, hitting

her hip hard and painfully against something sharp when the boat threw her down.

She felt terrible. Worse when she crawled out of the head and found Neil standing there, glaring at her. She could hear the anger in his voice, but she didn't care. She only wanted to escape this, to curl up somewhere quiet and still. Oh, lord, please . . . still and calm!

It hurt when he touched her head. It even hurt when he smoothed her hair back. Every nerve in her body was hypersensitive with painful nausea. Why didn't he do something to help her? How could a sticky piece of something behind her ear help when it was her stomach that cried for mercy?

She had to dash to the head again. He was gone when she came out, and she sank down to the floor, lying there in an agonised, helpless ball. Each time the bow ploughed into a wave, inertia pressed her body into the floor, then lifted it a second later. Under her, she could hear water sloshing in the fresh-water tanks, the sound amplifying her nausea.

After a while the motion seemed to ease a little. She lay very still, waiting for the violent surging to return. Minutes passed. She became conscious of herself, of how she would look if he came down. Lying on the floor in a disgusting heap. Did she dare to move? She was learning quickly that any motion tended to make the nausea worse.

He had suggested she would feel better up above. Did he really know? He hadn't looked even vaguely uncomfortable. He had crouched there beside her, the boat throwing her stomach into convulsions while he looked disgustingly healthy. Whatever had made her think he would be a good man to go to sea with? What had she been thinking of? She had never, in all her life, got herself into a mess like this!

She moved very carefully, hunched over, and managed to stand up in the head and wash her face and brush her teeth. She even used some of the mouthwash she found on a shelf and it didn't make her stomach convulse. When she was done she bent down and opened the door to put the mouthwash back, then the boat lurched and everything in the cupboard tumbled out the open door, crashing and flying everywhere.

Her hands flew out to stop the disaster, but her reactions seemed muted, slow, and she ended up standing helpless, staring at the chaos, feeling the nausea returning and knowing she would never manage to get all that picked up without being sick again.

'Go on up and sit in the cockpit.' His hand on her shoulder was gentle, although his face when she turned was rigid. What was he suppressing? Anger? Disgust?

'I'll pick it——'

'Get outside before you get sick again. I'll clean this up!' His head jerked, and it was anger. She went. She was far too sick to do anything else.

She almost fell in the companionway as the boat threw her to starboard, but the walls were so close beside her that she remained on her feet. She held on tight as she went up the steps, then collapsed on to the seat in the cockpit, her head resting on a hard, cold winch.

Slowly, amazingly, she realised that the motion had become almost soothing. *Passagemaker* surged forward into each wave, reared back as she was lifted, yet always forward. She could feel the wind in her hair and the coolness of the metal winch felt wonderful, although it dug into her cheek with each wave.

She shifted, leaning back, opening her eyes warily, but the nausea remained at a low level, almost bearable. Neil was still down below, cleaning up the mess she had made. The guilty muscles in her body started to move her to her feet, but she sank back into her corner, unwilling to face the nauseous motion below.

All around her, white tops of racing waves were popping through the darkness. The sails were curved hard, pushed out to the port side of the boat, pushing them over. No wonder she had trouble walking down below. They were tilted over, held by the wind as they ploughed into the waves.

She jumped as a loud bang exploded on the far side of the boat. A wall of white spray shot up, thrown back over her head, wet, salty water slapping her face.

'Feeling better?' His head emerged, then the rest of him, bulky in a yellow suit that seemed to puff out everywhere. She wished he would sound a little friendlier. This man was a stranger, a world away from the dark-skinned man who had smiled at her on Monday night.

'Yes, a little better.' Should she have said that? What if he expected her to move, to do some kind of work? She dreaded what motion might do to her stomach. She watched him checking everything, his eyes taking in the set of the sails, the numbers on the compass, then a quick glance back into the navigation cabin, and she knew he had taken in the course on the Loran, the image on the radar screen. 'I'm sorry about the mess. I——'

'Forget it. Here, move over to the other side for a second.' She moved, sensing his impatience, her limbs responding slowly, as if she were drugged. He uncleated the line from a winch. The rope creaked as he let it slide out a few inches and the white foresail responded instantly, popping out harder, fuller, to port. The whole boat shifted, leaned harder into the waves. 'That's better. We'll pick up a bit more speed.'

The moonlight was enough to see weary lines stretched from the corners of his eyes. Her gaze followed the lines to the windblown chaos of his hair, suppressed an urge to touch and smooth them away with her fingers.

'It was clumsy of me,' she admitted. 'I should have thought when I opened the cupboard——'

'Forget it.' He was looking forward, tossing the words back. 'I keep telling myself I'll put a lee rail in the damned cupboard, and I keep forgetting to do it.' Was the impatience in his voice for himself, or for her? He turned and settled himself in the cockpit seat, and she could see him well enough then to know it was Serena Jones who had put the rough tones in his voice. 'How long does it last?'

'What?' Her stupidity, did he mean? Her clumsiness? 'It's time for my watch, isn't it? I——' She broke off, terrified at the thought of him going to sleep, leaving her alone with the wind and the sea and the night.

'Past time for your watch,' he snapped, then he sighed and his voice softened, but she could hear the effort behind his simulated patience. 'I'll get us past Tatoosh Light and on course, then you can have the watch. But you better stay up here or you'll be sick again. How long does it last, anyway?'

'What?' She still didn't understand, and that was probably her fault, but he spoke so quickly and her mind was molasses.

'When does the seasickness usually subside? A

day? Two days?' Her fingers fluttered towards the patch adhered to the skin behind her ear. 'That doesn't work for everyone, you know. It's pretty good, but if it doesn't work——Last year, how long were you sick? Why the hell didn't you take something this time?' He frowned, then snapped, 'I don't suppose it makes any difference, but I'd like an idea of how long it's going to be before I can get a decent sleep. I can probably get through until tomorrow night with just cat naps, but——'

'I don't know.' She heard the whimper in her voice and hated herself for it. She was beginning to realise the seriousness of what she had done. It wasn't just the fact of lying to him, but this man *needed* competent help, and she was virtually useless to him.

'Surely last time—how long was it last year?'

'It wasn't—I didn't—last year I wasn't sick.' She knew she must tell him sooner or later, but she would have preferred a moment when there was some kindness in his face, softness in his voice. She swallowed and worked on lining up the right words.

'How the——' He shook his head as if he weren't hearing correctly. 'Last year you said there was strong winds and a gale. How could you be sick now and not——'

She could see the moment when he realised, when the frustration changed to understanding. He seemed to relax farther back into the corner where he sat, his arm hooking over the winch behind him for balance as the boat surged and rocked against the wind and waves.

All right. She was ready for it. She deserved it, and there was no point trying to put it off until she felt better and his temper was smoother. He would probably shout at her, and she deserved that, but she was certain he was not a man who would hit a woman.

'Neil, I . . .' She wished that there was land, a dock, some way to take her medicine, listen to him having his say, then run, get the hell off his boat and away from everything—the nausea, the panic, the man.

'Sorry, Serena.'

Was she hearing right? What had *he* to apologise for? She was the one who had done the unforgivable, representing herself as good crew when she was inexperienced and incompetent. For heaven's sake, the man sounded almost embarrassed as he said, 'I really didn't think of it.'

'It?'

What the hell did he mean? She shifted erect, staring at him, vaguely surprised that she could sit straight without feeling too wildly sick. 'What didn't you think of?'

He shook his head, looked even more uncomfortable and finally said, 'I had no intension of embarrassing you, Serena. I just didn't think about—that you're a woman.'

'Of course I'm a woman.' She giggled, but it was a nervous sound. He had known she was a woman the first time their eyes met. She remembered the shock of what had to have been a strong, crazy, mutual physical attraction.

He was nodding, and she decided that he must be a little insane. Then he said, 'I should have realised that—well, I suppose some women would be more susceptible to seasickness at certain times of the month.'

'You think I've got my period?' Her words were out before she really thought, and she felt the surge of heat, embarrassment, because it wasn't the sort of

thing she normally threw into conversation with anyone, much less a man. Again, she felt a strong urge to
laughter, nervous giggling. She forced it down, her
throat making a funny, choking gurgle as she
managed, 'I——'

'I'll check our position,' he said hurriedly, getting
up and ducking into the after cabin all in one quick
motion, leaving her outside alone, her words, confession or whatever, dying into nothing.

He had given her an excuse for her behaviour. She
would be a horrible coward if she took advantage of
his embarrassment and accepted it, but—looking
around her at the size of the dark waves, at the dark
violence of breaking white crashing against the side
of the boat, she realised that, yes, she *was* a coward.
She was a flaming wimp, a disgusting disgrace to her
sex and her country. If she were on dry land, safe,
she might be able to face his contempt at her
confession, but out here—no! She simply could not
do it.

He stayed below for a long time. She looked back
once or twice, saw the back of his head bend in
concentration over the chart, saw the green picture
on the radar screen. She might pick this up, after all.
The radar picture made some sense. She could
recognise the shape of the exit from Juan de Fuca
Strait. It was not all that different from the way it
looked on a map: the bottom shore of Vancouver
Island on one side, with the north coast of
Washington curving up towards Canada. Only, on
the radar, *Passagemaker* was at the centre of the
picture, on a course for a spot just north of the
lighthouse. If she looked ahead, she could see the
light. Tatoosh Lighthouse. The last land she would
see for days.

She shivered, surprised at how cold the air was out here on the water. In Victoria, the nights had been warm with the heat of summer, but this was cold like winter. She would have to go below for a heavier sweater. Hopefully she could make it without her stomach getting hysterical again.

She closed her eyes while she thought about going down for warmer clothes, then somehow she was jerking awake to the touch of firm fingers on her shoulder. 'Serena, you'll have to move. I've got to get at the lines to work the sails.' He pushed an orange bundle into her arms. 'Put that on. You'll be warmer.'

The cruiser suit was far too large for her, but she sat in the cockpit, trying to stay out of his way and not really succeeding, pulling on the padded suit. The suit he wore was yellow, but this one was orange. A slightly different style, but just as big and bulky and awkward. It zipped up and it provided instant protection from the cold wind, but she would be tripping on it if she tried to move.

'Here, do these up.' He was bending at her feet. She looked down at him, caught her crazy hand as it reached to tame that wild blond hair. What was he doing to her? Right now he was doing up some kind of fastener that tightened the legs of the suit at her ankle, making it billow out above the strap. But what was he doing to her body, the woman part of her that had not stirred for so long?

It would have been better, safer, to pursue these feelings at home, on dry land, where she could get away, get her breath, and feel some control of what was happening.

'How do you feel?' He rocked back on to his heels. He was only inches away from her, his face clear in the light from the aft cabin.

'OK. Not bad now. I think if I stay out here, I'll be all right.' He was still watching her, trying to read things she hoped were well hidden. 'I—do you want me to take the watch now?'

He nodded. 'We're on a good course to clear everything. We're clear of the reef now.' She had not known there was a reef. 'I've plotted our course on the chart. So if you can handle it . . .? Just give the autopilot a nudge if it seems to be drifting off, and watch the radar for other boats.'

She looked past him, the instruments, the chart. What was there that she should know, that she would have to do while he slept? She felt guilty at the gentle patience in his voice. Somehow his crazily incorrect analysis of her actions had stirred the protective male in him. The man was tired, getting exhausted, and if she said she could not handle the watch he would stay up and do it for her. How could she take advantage of him like that?

'There are no other reefs? Nothing to hit?' She swallowed. 'What if the wind shifts? Do you—should I——' He looked so tired. He had said he was tired last night, and he had been up so early, getting them underway. Now, unexpectedly, his lips curved and he laughed.

'Not a thing to hit. We're clear of it all. Just watch for traffic on the radar. Wake me up if you're not sure. The sails should be OK. If the wind swings more to the north, just alter course a little more to the west. A few more miles of westing won't hurt anything. There's nothing out there but Hawaii. I'll trim sail when I relieve you. Wake me up at four.'

Hawaii. It was an uncomfortable thought, all those miles and miles of ocean. She had a long time to think about it, crouched in the cockpit, staring at the dark sky and the white phosphorescence of the waves.

If she craned her head around the door to the aft cabin, she could see Neil's legs sprawled under his sleeping-bag. She had heard him taking his clothes off: the rustle of the cruiser suit, then the denim sliding down over his thighs as his jeans joined the cruiser suit. She had swallowed, hearing and knowing he was stripping. She had stared so hard at the white, breaking waves. What was getting into her? Next, she would be sneaking into newsagents to buy *Playgirl* magazines!

How could she even think about a man that way when she was out here alone? She was terrified that the wind would suddenly and violently change, but the sails stayed filled and, although the instruments in front of her showed that the wind had picked up a few knots, nothing terrible happened. After a while she relaxed. It simply wasn't possible to maintain that kind of terror forever.

Earlier, while she had been dozing in the cockpit, Neil must have taken the reef out of the main. It was pulled up right to the top of the mast now. They had turned enough to be running with the wind, an easier course to sail.

Three hours. She had not realised how sleepy she was, how long three hours could be. She should get up and move around, but she was a little afraid of movement, terrified to actually go out on to that heaving deck and leave the protection of the cockpit. Yet she kept drifting off, jerking awake with her eyes flying to the radar. She had to move, to keep awake.

She climbed into the after cabin, moving carefully, hanging on to keep herself from flying everywhere as the boat rocked wildly on a big wave. How did Neil do it, sliding quickly through that doorway and down the steps as if everything were stable and quiet?

He was there, his arm thrown across his forehead. She could see the bulge of his shoulder muscles smoothed by sleep. His lips were parted slightly, softened. She watched his chest moving, the sprinkling of fair hairs above the top of the sleeping-bag. He was deeply asleep, despite the slight shifting of his body as the waves surged under them.

It was impossible to wake a man sleeping so comfortably. She looked outside and knew that there was no reason. The boat was stable, the motion normal for the conditions. There was no reason to wake him except that she was alternating between sleeping and panicking.

Face it. The problems were all inside her head. She only wished that acknowledging that would make it easier. Why on earth had she wanted to do this? She should be at home reading an adventurous book and living her own wonderfully dull life. Could she possibly survive for six, seven, even eight days of nothing but constant motion and Neil Turner?

What if they sprang a leak and sank? Was the life raft in that canister any good? How long would they drift on angry waves before someone found them? What if she panicked totally, threw a screaming fit? What if the wind blew up into a gale? It was one thing to blithely tell him that she had been at sea during a gale last summer. The words had come out easily, but the real thing would be horrifying! Right now the waves were only about a meter high, but under them was a westerly swell that sometimes surged up forever. What if it got bigger and bigger, tossing them about like a toy?

She stumbled to the VHF radio and switched on the

weather channel, heard the calm voice of a coast-guard radio operator telling her that winds offshore would be north-westerly fifteen to twenty-five, with swell height of three to four meters developing by tomorrow morning.

There was no way she could do it. She licked her lips and turned to look at the sleeping man. She had to wake him up, to tell him it was no good. He had to take her back home. Turn around and go back, to land and wharfs and civilisation. Face it, she admonished herself, he would be better off alone than with someone as inexperienced as she was, as frightened as she was.

His arm slid away from his forehead, coming to rest against his hair on the pillow. The light from the chart table showed his eyelids closed, his face seeming very young and vulnerable. As she watched, his lids twitched uncomfortably in the light, then his body shifted, turning, curving so that the sleeping-bag fell away from his back and his face was in shadow again.

It was two-thirty in the morning. She bit her lip and knew she could not wake him before the time he had said. Four o'clock. Then she would tell him. She turned back to the chart and used the dividers to step off the miles back to Victoria. In another hour and a half they would be ten miles further along the course line. How many hours would it take to get from there to Victoria?

Quite a few, but at least they would be getting closer to land all the time. She put the dividers away and went back outside, and it was a little easier to look at the massive waves with the knowledge that by morning home would be getting closer, not more distant. If she had something to do while she waited, the next hour and a half might not seem forever.

She was not tired now. She sat on the low side of the cockpit and leaned her head back, watching the water, seeing a long way ahead in the moonlight when they rose up on each swell. It was amazing how you got used to the motion, because it did not seem quite so frightening right now. The rhythm was almost soothing, hypnotic . . .

She jerked up, her heart pounding. What was that? What sound, already fading from her consciousness as she woke? She had fallen asleep, but for how long? Her eyes flew to the sails, but everything seemed the same. The radar——

Her eyes never got as far as the radar screen. Through the open cabin door she could see two very masculine, very naked legs stretched out to the floor. The light over the chart table glistened on the sun-bleached covering of hair. As she watched she saw hands, naked arms reaching down, one bare foot lifting and sliding into stiff denim. Then the other leg. Suddenly, he was standing, surging up, coming into view, his jockey shorts hugging the unmistakable shape of a man. She jerked around, trying to see waves and stars overhead.

What time was it? She lifted her wrist, pushing back the orange sleeve of the cruiser suit, but there was nothing to see. Damn! Why hadn't she bought a watch with a light on it, so she could press a button and see the time? Had she slept through her shift? How long had it been?

'Hi!' He took in everything else before he smiled at her, but the smile was there. 'Just let me wash and I'll take over while you get some sleep.' He had not put the cruiser suit on yet. She could see the muscles moving through his shirt as he pulled open the door to the forward part of the boat. He turned back to her just before his head disappeared down the hatch, his voice caressing as he said, 'Thanks, Serena. I needed the extra sleep badly.'

The hatch slid closed behind him and she could see the chronometer in the after cabin now. It was five o'clock. She had slept for over two hours, and he was thanking her, thinking she had done something special for him. If he only knew! Until sleep had claimed her she had been counting every second, just waiting for the moment she could wake him and tell him she could not go one mile further out into this ocean!

She waited now, her stomach fluttering, mostly from nervousness. As soon as he came back she would tell him, come clean and confess everything. He wouldn't like it, but he'd have to accept it, wouldn't he? Then she would sleep away the next few hours, and after that she'd just put up with his anger. After all, it was only until they got back to Victoria.

What was taking him so long down there? Wash, he had said, but he had been—how long? At least ten minutes now. What would be the best way to tell him? Could she explain about Terry? She had to give some reason, and couldn't possibly explain that, while Terry had got her to the party, it was Neil's magnetism that had drawn her on to this boat. The man had hit her like a ton of bricks, the first male since the early days with Terry to make her remember she was a woman, a sensual creature.

The hatch slid forward. She caught the aroma of coffee, her stomach twisting in a spasm that told her the seasickness was nowhere near over. Then Neil emerged, a steaming mug in each hand. He held one out to her and she took it, avoiding breathing in the horrid smell of the coffee. He opened the door, holding it so it would not bang as he slid out into the cockpit.

'I was going to get you coffee, but I thought it might not go too well if you're still feeling sick. So I made a bit of soup instead.' He lifted his own mug of coffee and sipped it, obviously enjoying it. She eased the mug closer, smelled a mild beef broth. She drew in the aroma and it seemed pleasant. When she sipped, it was hot. She tried another sip and the liquid slipped down. It felt good.

'Thank you. It's lovely.' She smiled at him and she felt warm when he smiled back. They sat together quietly. She had checked the course while they were below, and was relieved to find that while she had slept the autopilot had kept them going in the right direction. The numbers on the Loran matched up as they should.

He was obviously not a man who talked a lot on first waking. He seemed very content, watching everything in a lazily observant way. When he drained the last of the coffee he seemed to shift into gear, putting the cup down into a holder and sitting forward so that she sat a little straighter too.

'Everything fine while I slept?' She nodded guiltily and he said, 'Yes, I can see it was.' He grinned, glancing back at the radar. 'We're almost out of the shipping lanes now.'

Her eyes followed and saw nothing at all. It took her a second to realise that the radar was turned on, but that the land was too far away now for its twelve-mile range. How far offshore? She wanted to ask, but she should be the one to know. *She* had been on watch.

'You'd better go below and get some sleep.' She nodded, but did not move. It was time now. She still didn't know how to tell him, but she had better get the words moving before she lost her nerve.

'Neil, I want to tell you that——'

'No, just hold on a second, will you?' He was on his feet, the wind moulding his shirt so that she could see how the muscles bulged, how his abdomen was flat and hard. What would it be like if she touched him there, her fingers tracing the hard curves? Would he tremble if she——?

She shuddered and jerked herself straighter, then she stood up because that was motion at least, and she could look away and pretend that the waves and the lightening sky were fascinating.

'Just keep an eye on me while I trim the sail, will you? We're far enough out that we could make more southing, and it would be a little more comfortable.' He quickly freed a line from the cleat and handed it to her. 'Here, take that line. Let it out when I tell you.'

He grabbed his harness and clipped the safety line to the rope that led from the bow to the stern. Then she watched him go forward on the heaving deck, his safety line slipping along with him. He had some kind of tackle in his hands now, and he was rigging it around the boom of the mainsail.

'OK, let her out now!'

She let the rope slip through her hands. The main boom swung far out to the side, then lifted and started to swing back as a wave surged under them. He pulled the tackle tight before the boom could swing, then called, 'OK, take her south about fifteen degrees!'

She turned the control for the autopilot past three

of the little marker lines. The boat swung and the wind seemed to lighten as it shifted behind them. Neil joined her, but did not shed his safety line. There was no criticism in his face, so hopefully she had done everything right.

She didn't make any motion to go below, and he sat beside her. 'Nervous of going below? Afraid you'll get sick again?' She nodded, because that was certainly true, although it wasn't what was bothering her at this moment. *Neil, please turn back. Take me home.* He didn't hear her thoughts, although on Monday night she had thought he could read her mind. Now he pushed his hair back and said, 'Why don't you bunk down in my berth? It's the most comfortable sea berth on the boat, far less motion than up forward.'

She caught her lip between her teeth. Now was the time. She wished she didn't feel quite so scared of telling him. 'Neil, I—I know you needed someone efficient to crew on this trip. I'm sorry, but——'

He reached his hand out, his fingers touching her lips. 'Don't, Serena.' He shook his head slightly, not smiling, but his face softer. 'I think I'm the one who should be apologising. I'm afraid I was pretty lacking in understanding earlier. I'm afraid I'm not at my best when I'm short of sleep, but that's no excuse for me being so unsympathetic. Fortunately, I've never been seasick, but I should have realised much earlier that you were suffering. I thought——' He shrugged, and she wondered what it was that he was not going to say.

He shifted and he was closer, then incredibly his lips were touching hers, a fleeting, gentle kiss that somehow brought tears to her eyes. She swallowed, her lips trembling as his moved away. His hands took her shoulders and drew her to her feet. She moved, coming where his fingers guided.

She was standing very close, waiting for his arms, his lips on hers again. Her heart was panicking then still with waiting and needing. Her eyes seemed to be locked to his, although they were out of the light and there were only shadows and a sweet, heavy wildness growing inside her.

His fingers slid down along the arms of the bulky cruiser suit she wore, then he whispered, 'Go to sleep, love. It's my watch now.' His hands gave her a gentle push and then she was inside without stumbling or falling against anything.

She knew her fingers were trembling as she undid the cruiser suit. She was terribly aware of him only a foot away. Then he went forward, and she knew he was giving her privacy to undress and get into bed.

She took off her jeans and, after hesitating, her sweater. Then she climbed into the bunk in her panties and bra and felt the warmth from him still lingering there.

CHAPTER FOUR

SERENA tried to catch at sleep again, but this time it would not work. Awareness was all through her—the sounds of the water rushing past the hull of the boat with incredible volume.

He had been in the cabin several times while she slept. She had half woken, keeping her eyes closed, her body turned away from him, listening to the sounds as he worked with the chart, the little beeps as he touched the controls of the Loran. She remembered how she had watched him in his sleep, and was careful to keep the sleeping-bag high over her shoulder.

Twice now she had woken with the sun bright across the sleeping-bag. This time she opened her eyes, turned her head and found the cabin empty. She looked through the little window at the head of the bunk and found the cockpit empty as well.

Where was he? She lay very still, straining to hear a sound that could be Neil. Nothing. The water. The wind. The half-angry flapping of the flag he flew from the stern.

What if he had fallen overboard while she'd slept? She leapt up, stumbling in the sleeping-bag. If he had fallen over, how would she ever know where to look for him? Back behind them, but how far? Could she spot him in all those big waves?

Surely he would not leave her all alone out here! She grabbed the edges of the doorway and pushed herself out, looking back desperately and seeing nothing but great, dark monsters of waves seeming to race after them. One loomed up behind, towering. She was certain it would bury the back of the boat in white foam. Then, at the last minute, the boat rose up, riding high, heeling wildly as it came down into the canyon between waves.

How could she turn the boat in that? How could she manage the wildness of handling sail as she turned to go upwind and search? How the devil did you start the engine on this beast? Why didn't she know that? Why hadn't he told her? Her fingers were aching from their desperate grip on the doorway. She forced herself to relax, heard a noise and jerked her head forward.

She felt a wild, sickening surge of relief. He was there, walking towards her from the front of the deck, crouching low against the motion, then standing erect as he grasped one of the steel shrouds. She could see the flat nylon line that attached his harness to the safety line.

He paused when he saw her, his body unconsciously moving slightly to compensate for the boat's motion. Despite the bright morning sun, he was not wearing his dark glasses. His eyes were narrowed against the glare from the water. For a long, frozen moment she was held by his intense gaze. Then the world surged in—waves and water and her own body, almost naked with only the skimpiest of coverings, a lace bra and panties. For a frozen moment she did not move, waiting, a wild part of her welcoming this inevitable moment.

Then self-consciousness surged over her, a wild tide of embarrassment. She ducked down, pushing the door closed with a bang, grabbing for her clothes.

She had never pulled on jeans and sweater so quickly in her life! As soon as she was covered, she shot back out of the after cabin, emerging barefoot in the cockpit, needing to replace that look in his eyes with something more ordinary.

'I——' She was breathless, her voice hardly audible. 'I thought you'd fallen over! I woke up, and I couldn't see you or hear you anywhere.' She lurched and grabbed for the side of the cockpit, and his hand caught around her waist at the same time, holding her against him securely.

Above her, his strong voice said, 'I never go on deck without my harness at sea. I want you to wear one, too, while I'm sleeping. Even in the cockpit.'

She nodded. She wasn't going to argue about safety measures. There was a terrifying amount of motion now. She watched, horrified, as a towering wave bore down on them, sending *Passagemaker* riding high and wild.

He laughed. 'Some of those suckers are big, aren't they?' She couldn't believe it, but the man was actually enjoying this! She looked up at him, feeling his hard strength all along her. His eyes were dark brown, warm lights in them as he looked down and said in a suddenly unsteady voice, 'How long did you say you could stay in San Francisco?'

'A week,' she whispered, her heart totally out of control. If he would keep his arms around her, maybe she could make it to San Francisco.

'A week,' he repeated gruffly, then he said in an odd voice, 'Will you spend that week with me?' She felt her head move, a silent assent, and she wondered what she was promising this man, and how she was going to survive the days between now and San Francisco. What did she really know about him?

Survive the Savage Sea. She seemed to remember that as the title of a book Terry had enjoyed, but it was horribly fitting to her current predicament. Neil might have held her in his arms, safe and strong, but she hadn't been awake for twenty minutes before he was in his bunk, sleeping, and she was alone with the sun high overhead and not another living thing in sight.

Except the seagulls.

She managed her watch a little better this time. She was terrified of the thought of going on deck, but she did not have to do that. Neil had forbidden her to leave the cockpit while he slept. She was to wake him if sail-handling was needed. Fine! This was one time when she was not going to complain about chauvinism. A woman would be insane to insist on the right to tend sail with the ocean crazy and the boat moving like a wild thing.

She concentrated on getting familiar with the instruments. She even managed to keep track of their course on the chart, trembling as she drew the course line in. Farther and farther from shore. She took down the dividers and measured, and they were sixty miles from the coast of Washington state, and still they headed out farther.

Out of the shipping lanes. She knew the logic. Away from the freight that moved up and down the coast, a sailing ship was safe. Nothing to hit. No rocks. No shallows. No other boats. Nothing to worry about, except the pull she felt, the desperate desire to grab that autopilot control and give it a big twist to the left.

If they headed directly for shore it would be almost a day before they got out of this everlasting nothing of water! She suspected it would be a terrible day if they tried to sail east with those big swells rolling down from the north.

The wind was stronger, which was probably why the waves were such monsters. They were moving at eight knots, an impressive speed for a sail-boat under reduced sail. While she'd slept, Neil had double reefed the mains'l, presumably in response to the increased winds. The wind and the waves and the boat were all going more or less in a southerly direction, so there wasn't the noisy slamming of water on the bow, the explosion of spray under the rub rails.

She was still frightened, but was beginning to believe that this boat could handle what the ocean was doing to it. She had no confidence at all in her own abilities to respond to the boat's demands, but Neil was close by, and he would wake if she needed him. All she really had to do was watch and keep track of their progress.

It became an endless cycle. Watch, then sleep. She hardly ever felt hunger, but Neil usually made soup when he got up, bringing her soup and crackers. The soda crackers seemed to settle her stomach, and were welcome because she still felt a mild seasickness. She never went forward except to use the head. She was uncomfortably aware that she was not pulling her weight on this trip, but thankfully he made no complaint. She slept in his bed, drawing comfort from his warmth, falling asleep quickly as the sleeping-bag came up over her shoulders.

Sometimes it seemed unreal that she had promised him a week in San Francisco. Everything was unreal except this. Four hours on. Four hour off. Night and day. The waves were big, but the winds dropped on the second day and the motion became more erratic without the wind to drive the boat forward.

Another watch, then another. She learned that four hours on watch exhausted a person, that her eyes drooped as she shared a mug of soup with Neil in the cockpit. Yet she treasured the warm closeness of those moments together before she went to bed. In the half-hour as they changed watches, they talked. It was easy talking to him. She found herself telling him about the kids in her class, her parents, even about her childhood fantasy of trading life as an only child for life in a big family.

He did not mention San Francisco again, but it was in his eyes. His lips never came near hers, not since that last time, and his fingers only touched when he reached to wake her. But when the passage was over, their relationship would change. It was a promise she hugged to herself, acknowledging that she was ready now to reach out, to take a chance, and that this man was a man worth reaching for.

She was learning about him, bits and pieces that filled out the skeleton of his life she had read in the log. He did not talk about himself, but she got him to talk about his family. His son was sixteen, looked more like his mother than his father. He had two brothers, twins two years older than him. Zeb was the strong one, the dependable one. Barry was the black sheep of the family, the trouble-maker. She decided that Neil was a little of both his brothers. Strong, yet volatile too.

His father had died when he was eighteen, but his mother was still alive. The boys all looked after their mother, and Serena read enough behind his words to know that mother was a clinging woman who leaned hard on her sons. Well, they were strong men, and there was enough traditional chauvinism in Neil's

voice and his words that she suspected he didn't
resent being leaned on. She wondered what it would
be like to make a life with a strong man.

She was not sure what there would be for her after
this trip. A week, but then what? Would she have
earned the right to greet him at some party years
from now, like the woman Gail? She hoped it was
more, because she was not a girl for giving lightly,
and he was a man who seemed to penetrate to her
soul. Yet she knew she had to go on. The time for
running had been when their eyes had first met, back
at that party.

He was most comfortable talking about the small
town in Mexico where he had developed a marina
and had plans for expanding it. Sometimes he talked
about Keith, but the boy was an uncomfortable topic
for him. Keith had been taking lessons by correspon-
dence for four years; first at sea during their circumnavigation, then in Mexico.

'He's done well,' Neil said slowly, his eyes
narrowed with worry. 'Good marks, and he's usually
ahead of schedule. He has a lot of friends, good kids,
so I'm not worried about the social aspect of his living
away from his native country. He's made friends
everywhere. Tahiti. Australia. Mexico.' He laughed,
said, 'Friends in three languages.'

'But?' she asked softly, because the concern was
there in his voice.

He tried to shrug it away, sipping his mug of soup.
When the soup was gone, his fingers were restless on
the mug. 'I suppose it's the usual teenage thing. He
hasn't shown much sign of rebellion until this last
year, but——' He moved uncomfortably on the
cockpit seat. 'We're not getting along the way we
were. Damn it, Serena, I swore I wouldn't make any

of the mistakes my father did, but we're getting into the same stupid arguments I had with my father when I was a kid.' His voice was frustrated. 'He wants to go to school in California this year. Maybe he should. He's getting into subjects where he should have school facilities. Computers, chemistry, that kind of thing. I don't want to hold him back. But damn it, the kid's only sixteen! I can't just let him go!'

'What else could you do? Move back to California?' It caught at something deep inside her when he looked like that, too vulnerable for the strong man she knew he was.

'I don't know.' He put the mug down, picked it up again. He didn't want to talk about this, yet could not seem to stop himself. 'Keith could go to boarding-school. Or he could stay with Zeb. That's what he wants to do. He's got a case of hero-worship for his uncle, and I should be glad of that because Zeb's certainly not going to lead him astray. But—damn it, Serena, I really will miss the kid!'

'What about moving back to California?'

He tossed the hair back, shrugged awkwardly. 'There's not much for me there. Oh, I could work in the family business. That's what I did before——'

Before Sandra died, she knew he meant. He pushed his hair back from his forehead, then finally ignored it when it promptly flopped forward again. 'It's not really my style. Zeb has it under control, and he's——' Neil grimaced ruefully. 'We're close, Zeb and I, so long as we don't work too closely. Then we clash, because he's always careful. The boat-building operation in San Diego is well-established. There isn't a lot of scope for taking chances, for wild new ideas.'

'So you'll stay in Mexico?'

'I don't know.' He couldn't sit still any longer. He leaned forward and picked up the stays'l sheet from its cleat, re-coiled it and put it back. Make work, she thought with faint amusement. 'I'm making up my mind every day, and the answer is never the same. I love my place in Mexico, and I've started something there. I've got about twenty local people employed now. I don't know what would happen to it all if I left. It's part of the family business, of course, so we'd hire someone to look after it, but it might not be the same. In a way, I even owe it to Zeb to stay there. He backed me when I started it.'

'Conservative Zeb?' It must have been a bit of a flier for an established firm and a careful man.

'Well, my brother has his moments. When I approached him—actually, I thought he'd laugh at me, but he didn't. Barry did, which kind of surprised me because he's never hesitated to take chances himself. I can consider it lucky that Keith didn't decide to worship Barry.'

'You've got a lot of family.'

She must have sounded wistful, because he said, 'You and Terry didn't have children?'

She played with the zipper of her cruiser suit. 'We were going to have kids later. We got married when we finished university. We were going to teach for five years, then go sailing for a couple of years. Then——' She bit her lip, because it always seemed so sad that Terry's dreams had all come to nothing. 'But he got sick, and none of it happened. All the dreams. He just didn't have a chance.'

His hand covered hers, the cool fingers warming her. 'He had that one trip,' he said softly. 'Your trip to San Francisco last year.'

'No.' She stared at his fingers, so still on her head. She swallowed. She had to say it, because this lie was a barrier she must pull down. 'I made it up. We—it was the plan. We were saving up. If—if Terry hadn't got sick, we'd have tried to find a crewing position last summer. Then this year we'd do it on our own boat. But none of it happened at all.'

He was very silent. She stared at a piece of dirt on the cockpit floor. How did dirt get there when they were miles and miles from shore? 'I lied about it, Neil,' she said, because he didn't seem to realise what she had just said. When her words penetrated, he would take his hand away and there would be a horrible distance between them again.

'You never went sailing at all?' He was speaking very carefully, as if he must get this clear.

Her fingers twitched under his and she bit her lip again, said huskily, 'The first couple of years, before he got sick—we sailed then. A friend of Terry's had a boat, and we went out at weekends.' She wanted to turn her hand and close her fingers on his, but she was afraid. She swallowed, admitted, 'In Georgia Strait. That's all. Never out on the open ocean. After that, when Terry was sick, it was just sailing magazines, books. Not the real thing.'

She made herself look up at him then. There was a funny half-smile on his face, but she didn't trust it. When it really sank in, he would be angry. Of course he would be angry.

He said softly. 'You conned me?'

'Not exactly. I—I never meant to——'

'Damn it, Serena! At the beginning I thought——Why?' His dark eyes had flared to black fire and she shivered under his questions.

'I didn't . . . It wasn't really deliberate.' The

reasons were too personal, too mixed up. 'It was such a funny night, and—that horrible man got my back up, so I lied about the trip. To them. I—it was crazy, childish, but I wanted to show him up. I—I never meant to go crewing with *anyone*. The party was just—I was sort of saying goodbye to Terry. I—and then you——'

He was frowning now, glowering. 'You said it was the anniversary of Terry's death.' He sighed and the anger seemed to drain out of him. 'I think I understand.'

Did he? He thought it was something she was doing for Terry. The party had been that, in the beginning, but not this. From that first shocking eye-contact, this man had overshadowed everything else. She could not explain, could not tell him that *he* was the reason she was here.

CHAPTER FIVE

AFTER that, when Neil looked at her his eyes were different. Serena felt like a stranger to him, as if he were a man she'd just met, a man who tolerated her because she was there.

He started explaining things about the boat now that he knew how green she was, but when he woke her at the end of his watch he used his voice, not fingers brushing her shoulder through the sleeping-bag. There was nothing she could do. She deserved this. She deserved much more and did not really understand why his voice had not risen in anger, why he had not shouted curses at her. She wished he *had* got angry, because his temper was quick and hot and just as quickly over.

The wind came up again the next day. She had lost track of the hours and the days, but that morning in the ship's log Neil had written the date. August the ninth. They had been at sea for four days. Sometimes she thought it was forever, although she had lost her fear now.

They were a hundred and twenty miles offshore by this time. 'Far enough,' Neil decided, changing their course at midday so that they would run parallel to the coast of Oregon.

During the night they crossed the imaginary line that separated the coast of Oregon from the coast of California. She logged the event, if it could be called an event, then went back outside. It was still terribly

cold at night, and it seemed unbelievable that
northern California was due east.

Through the darkest hours of the night the wind
rose slowly, the sails straining ahead, then seeming
to ease as the boat picked up speed. She watched, a
little nervous at first of the creaking lines, the
changing sounds as their speed increased. Then she
relaxed, realising that everything seemed to be all
right. Their ship had taken life again, the light winds
were over. She felt a warm happiness at the world,
the stars and the waves—everything was as it should
be.

She had lost her panic at not seeing land anywhere.
Now it seemed a safe thing: no land, no dangers. Just
the wind and the waves and Neil. Everything she
needed, if he would only come to relax with her
again. She watched the way the sails loved the wind,
and imagined his pleasure when he woke. She went
inside and plotted their position, pleased that their
speed had picked up from three knots to six. She
could hear the water boiling past the hull and it was
wonderfully exciting.

She would be terrified if she were alone. Thank
goodness he was careful, because she would be a
basket case if anything happened to him and she was
left alone out here. She hadn't done anything except
navigation and handling lines in the cockpit to his
instructions. Frankly she had no desire to tend sails,
although she was going to start helping him in the
galley today. There was no reason why she could not
do that. The galley was securely indoors and her seasickness was truly gone now.

At four in the morning she went down and daring-
ly touched his bare shoulder with her fingers. His
hand closed over hers and held it, and she sat very

still on the side of his bunk, looking down at his darkened form, feeling a deep joy that had nothing to do with sex. She had not touched him since confessing her deception. She was glad now that she had reached out.

'Everything OK?' he asked, his voice shedding sleep.

'Fine. We've got wind again.' Her fingers tingled against the warmth of his shoulder.

'I can tell that.' There was a smile in his voice. I've been lying here, listening to it. We must be doing about six knots.'

'Six point two,' she corrected happily. 'And I've made coffee for you.' She was still not drinking coffee herself. She would leave that until she was back on dry land and did not have to think about seasickness returning.

He caught her hand and brought it to his mouth. She felt his lips touch right through her. Then he released her and she could feel the energy starting to surge through him, and he said gently, 'Move, love, and I'll get up.'

'Don't you ever laze in bed?' she asked, laughing, standing up and trying not to look as if her flesh was trembling from a light kiss.

'Not when I'm alone in the bed.'

She went back to the cockpit, because she hadn't the nerve to tell him that she wanted to be in that bed *with* him, that her bloodstream was singing with the promise of his touch. She did not know how to say a thing like that to a man, and she was afraid to let him see how much he affected her.

It would be very easy to love this man, but she was not fooling herself that he would love her back. Her heart might stop when he called her 'love,' but he had used the same casual endearment for the girl collecting admissions at the party. He liked her, and he certainly *wanted* her, but all he had ever suggested they share was a week in San Francisco. She hugged that promise to herself, because she believed that San Francisco with Neil was going to happen. He still liked her, wanted her.

In all her life she had only had one lover, the man she'd married. Neil would probably never mention marriage, but she knew she would not draw back from him. He had family, a son and two brothers, as well as a mother who clung. But she was the only one he had ever talked to about his problems with Keith. Perhaps she was the only one who knew he was a sensitive, vulnerable man under the strength. There was a place in his life, an empty place she knew she could fill if he wanted her to.

She wanted to. She knew it was insane, for she had only known him for a few days, but if he asked she would walk into his life and stay on whatever terms he wanted. 'Love', she told herself softly, and the word was growing a meaning it had not had for her before, a wild excitement that had never penetrated her relationship with Terry.

He was frowning when he came into the cockpit. He did not make his usual trip forward to wash, but stood with his hands in his jeans pockets, his legs balanced astride, his teeth worrying his lower lip. Usually he leaned forward and picked up the cup of instant coffee she made for him, took it with him when he went to wash. Not this time. She felt her own tension growing with his.

'The wind's shifted,' he said finally, twisting to look over his shoulder. 'How long's it been like that?'

She hadn't noticed the flag flying from the opposite

side. The sails had stayed full, so she had never looked back. But now the wind was blowing from the north-east and the mains'l was sailing by the lee, set on the wrong side. The self-tacking stays'l had shifted to the port tack, but the main was held by the tackle Neil had put on to stop the boom slamming as they rode up over the big waves.

'I'm not sure how long it's been like that, Neil. I——'

The lines fanning out from his eyes were deep and worried. 'It doesn't look as if it's going to shift back. I'd better get that sail across.'

'What do you want me to do?' She did not fully understand what the problem was, but she felt his tension.

'Just stay in the cockpit.' He was rigging his harness as he spoke. 'When I release that preventer, the sail might come across with quite a force. I'll try to time it so it doesn't, but—just don't go out on deck, OK?'

'OK.' He picked up a coil of line and started forward, and she said breathlessly, 'Please be careful, Neil,' but he did not hear. It was silly anyway, because he was certainly careful whenever he went up to tend sails, never neglecting the safety harness.

The water seemed to go wild, as if maliciously preventing him from managing his task easily. She could see how the heaving deck was making it difficult for him to move. He got forward of the mast and she could see his legs under the boom of the mains'l. Then he was crouching down, his shoulders and arms building powerfully as he strained to release the tackle. She was terrified, watching, seeing the tremendous pressure on the tackle.

Why hadn't she noticed the shifting wind? She

should have been looking for it. She'd been out here, doing nothing, just sitting and enjoying the stars, thinking about how the ancient sailors must have spent hours finding archers and scorpions in the scattering of bright lights above their ships.

There was a crack, loud and sudden over the howling wind. Panic balled up in her chest and she cringed as she saw the wind catch the boom, lifting it high and out of control. She didn't know what the terrible noise had been, but her horrified eyes managed to locate Neil's legs, straight and braced against the deck, still standing. Then the world went wild, the boom flying across the deck, slamming out hard, the sail seeming to explode with a deafening crack as the wind pressed it against the shrouds.

The boat shifted, losing equilibrium, careening over a wave, down in the depths, then rising, surging, swinging. She was frozen, holding on, then she realised that she should do something, that the boat was swinging wildly back past its course, that the wind might get too far to starboard and actually catch that sail and send it crashing back the other way, and Neil . . .

She reached for the autopilot override, hesitated, her hand hovering, frightened of trying to tame the wild motions with her own hands on the wheel. It was steadying, wasn't it? Coming back on its own, the gyrations settling out. Yes, she was sure it was. Where was Neil?'

'Neil!'

Her scream was thrown back at her. She gripped the wheel with frozen fingers. Oh, heaven, please . . . Where——There he was! He had moved, was crouched over something on the foredeck. He was all right, doing something, some kind of fussing over

lines, tidying up the tackle, perhaps. She must learn
more about what went on up there.

It was all right. The compass was steadying at
about one hundred and sixty degrees, the course
Passagemaker had been making ever since last night.
Allowing for magnetic deviation, they were heading
almost due south. She let the wheel go, her hands
doing nothing to affect the steering because she had
never pushed the autopilot override.

Shouldn't he be coming back by now? He was still
there, not moving, just crouching on the foredeck.
Why hadn't he done anything about that line that
was streaming out to starboard? Why didn't he——?

He was not moving. He had been there too long,
not moving. Not crouched, but huddled. Hurt? Was
he hurt?

'Neil!' She stepped up on to the seat, starting on to
the deck. The top of a wave caught the boat and
threw her down, her hands grabbing desperately,
finding nothing, her leg crashing painfully down on
to the corner of the winch.

Safety harness. She was wearing one, as Neil had
commanded, but it wasn't connected to anything. A
second ago, when that wave had hit, if she had been
up on deck, she might have gone overboard! She
took the hook out of the pocket of her cruiser suit, got
it on to the jack line with trembling fingers . . . Neil!
Why didn't he get up?

He had moved, seemed to be lying down now. Or
had that sudden lurch thrown him down? What if—
what if he was dead? She felt a horrible pain deep in
her chest and she started up, hanging on to everything, her legs weak and trembling. It was terrible up
here, the waves so much closer, everything so
horribly unstable.

He was lying on the deck, his head resting on the skylight to her cabin, the one she never used. The crouching attitude was because he was still held by his harness. His eyes were closed. There wasn't anything she could call a sign of life. She got to him, huddled down and found herself held back by her harness.

'Please, Neil,' she whispered, the wind grabbing her voice. 'Don't be dead. Please!'

Would life do this to her always? Take away the people she loved? For she did love him. There had hardly been a chance, but it would have been the biggest thing in her life. He could have *been* her life.

She held on to the mast while she undid the snap to her safety harness, then she snapped it on to his. She didn't know if that was safe or not, but she could get closer now. Her fingers could probe, feel under his harness, push aside his shirt, her palm hard against his ribcage, pressing into the muscles and desperately trying to feel.

It wasn't her imagination, was it? There was movement, a heartbeat? She bent down, bracing herself not to fall into him, her face against his lips. 'Neil? Open your eyes. Please, be alive!'

She closed his nostrils with her fingers, covered his lips with hers. The kiss of life. She took a breath, ready to begin, but then she felt it, the soft, warm movement of air. He was breathing! He was alive!

'Neil?' His eyelids did not move. Oh, lord! What were the three things? Why hadn't she taken more first aid lessons? What was it? Heartbeat? He had that, hard and strong under her fingers. Breath? Yes!

Bleeding? Was he bleeding somewhere? She felt

desperately, her hands touching his body everywhere, her eyes searching for something. If he had broken anything, it did not show, did not reveal itself to her fumbling touch. There was no place where her hand came away wet with his blood, yet somehow he had hurt himself. He was alive, but why would he not wake up?

The radio!

She left him, releasing her safety harness and starting along the deck before she got it refastened. She must be more careful! She had to hurry, but if she went overboard they would both be lost, both gone.

'Mayday!' She gulped as she got the microphone to her lips. Was she on the right channel? Yes, the dial said sixteen. The emergency channel.

'Mayday, Mayday, Mayday. This is——' She took a deep breath, scatterings of the correct procedure remembered from a long-ago radio operator's course. 'This is the yacht *Passagemaker.*' Should she have left him while she went to the radio? Yes, she had to get help, but she should have covered him first. Warmth, the risk of shock. 'We're——' Her eyes flew to the Loran for her position, but her brain would not take in the numbers. 'We need the coastguard! Someone's hurt.'

Silence. She turned the squelch knob, but there was no answer hiding under the squelch level. She called again, organising her words better, but there was no answer. No coastguard. No boats.

Out of the shipping lanes, Neil had said. Out of radio contact, too. That hundred and twenty miles was too far for VHF radio. She went back to him, but his eyes were still closed. She tried to think how she could get him inside, but she knew that there was no way. He was too heavy. The sea was too rough. He simply had to stay here. She would have to make him comfortable somehow.

She started back again, ducking in terror as the boom lifted and started to swing towards her. She crouched, terrified, as it hovered, lifted high, the wind caught under the sail. Then it dropped and the sail popped back out to the side. She stumbled back to the cockpit and twisted the autopilot control, sending them twenty degrees or so farther to the east. Maybe it was the wrong course, but it would keep the wind firmly on the port side, keep that boom from swinging over and hitting her while she tried to look after Neil. They were far enough out to sea that she could worry about where she was going later.

What had happened? He hadn't been hit by the boom. She was sure he hadn't. Almost sure. He'd been very carefully standing behind it, where the shrouds kept the boom from swinging. But somehow he had fallen or been struck down as he was trying to release the tackle.

The tackle! She saw it then, the rope streaming out from the boom. She had wondered why he wasn't tending to that flying rope. Somehow it must have got away from him. Yes, because if he had finished the job the tackle would be fastened on the other side, keeping that boom from trying to fly across when the wind lifted it. Later. She would think about it later, figure out what she had to do.

She grabbed the microphone again, but when she called no one heard her. No answer. The radio was useless. She had to get him warm. That was more important right now.

Sleeping-bag. She grabbed it from his bunk and started forward, remembering this time to fasten her

safety line. She seemed to be foundering around,
jumping from one thing to the next. She had to get her
mind organised. First get him warm. The boat seemed
stable now that the course was changed, the wind
definitely on the port side. Time to get Neil warm, try
to move him somehow.

You weren't supposed to move an injured person,
but all that motion up on the foredeck couldn't be
good for him. His head was lying on that hatch,
pushing into it every time the bow surged up. She had
to get him off there, get him flat where he would not
be hurt even more by the wild rolling of the boat on
the waves. She had to get him back nearer the cockpit,
where the motion was less.

She spread out the sleeping-bag beside him, but
the wind caught it and she was fighting with it and
losing to the wind. Then she thought to tuck the
corners under the lines that ran along the deck,
control lines for the forward sails. There. It was
staying still.

She started to roll him, crouching behind him to
cushion his movement with her own body. He rolled
part of the way, then stopped. His safety line was
holding him back. She released it and quickly
reattached it to a shroud behind her. Then she pulled
the sleeping-bag around him, but was worried about
his head. There should be something under his head.
She went back, got a pillow and cushioned his head,
keeping her own safety line attached every minute.
She had to be careful. For him.

As her fingers slipped out from under his pillowed
head she felt the bump. No dampness, no bleeding,
just a thickening where something had hit him.

The tackle. It had come free somehow, that metal a
horribly lethal projectile flying on the end of the

rope. It had knocked him unconscious. She had to get him to hospital somehow, had to get a doctor. She went back again and tried the radio. No answer. Never any answer.

Back on deck. If she kept going back and forth on to the deck there would be an accident. All that motion, and those seconds while she undid her safety line to refasten it where she could reach Neil. She had to get him back to where she could look after him from the cockpit.

It took a long time. She thought about it while she went to bring in that flying rope. The tackle was still there, streaming out from the boom, and she had to be careful to get hold of it without being hit by a couple of pounds of heavy metal. Something must have broken, because the tackle was supposed to stay fixed to the deck, the rope sliding through it when he released it.

She got it in her arms, metal and rope. Then she got the other end free from the boom and took it back, threw it on to his bed in the after cabin. The pin that held the metal to the deck was gone; it must have broken under the strain.

She decided that she would drag him back, sliding him on the teak deck by pulling on the sleeping-bag. If she pulled him back along the port side, she should be able to get him wedged safely between the shrouds and the cockpit walls on the high side of the boat. He would be shielded from the wind and she could look after him without leaving the cockpit.

She worked it all out in her mind, but she tried the radio once more before she actually started moving him. It would be so much better if people came with helicopters and stretchers and professional competence. There was, of course, no answer, so she went back to Neil. The sleeping-bag had blown open and he was being chilled by the cold wind. She had to move him, and soon.

She had pulled Neil and the bag two feet when her burden stuck, jammed against the line crossing the deck. She couldn't drag him over it. She wanted to cry in frustration, but there was no one to help her if she broke down. She gritted her teeth and started tracing the line to find out what it was.

It was connected to the stays'l. In the end she decided that she would have to lower the sail to get the rope out of the way. Thankfully the stays'l was the smallest sail of them all! It came down quickly and she didn't bother to bundle it up properly, just grabbed a piece of rope and bunched it up roughly, let the wind play with the rough edges sticking out. Then she undid the rope from the foot of the sail and traced it along the deck, unthreading it from pulleys and eyes and coiling it up. There were no more barriers then and she walked backwards, pulling on the sleeping-bag and sliding him until he was wedged just where she wanted him. Then she could zip the bag up. He did not need the safety line here. He was wedged in securely between the shrouds and the cockpit sides.

He was still breathing, thank heaven! She thought his colour was a little better, but perhaps she had imagined that. Up on deck it had been darker, just the moonlight showing her his skin oddly pasty under the dark tan. Her fingers went to the lump on his head. She had turned his head before she started pulling him, to avoid putting pressure on that injury. She pulled back now before her fingers touched, afraid of hurting him.

'Please be all right,' she whispered, tears welling up to choke her voice. If only someone would answer the radio! How was she going to get him to a hospital?

She tried the radio again, but she had given up hoping for an answer. Then she went down into the after cabin and tried to figure out where the closest port was. She took the longitude and latitude from the Loran and plotted it on the chart. They were quite a bit north of San Francisco still, but far enough out to sea that heading for—say—Eureka would not save more than ten or twelve hours.

She went back out, tried the radio again, then checked the wind and tried to decide what they should do. What would Neil do if it was her lying there, helpless? They were on a comfortable course now, but if she tried to pull them further to the east, to head directly for Eureka, they would be broadside to the waves and close on the wind. It would be a horribly rough ride, and she was certain that the motion would not do his head injury any good. Why the devil did the wind and swell never seem to come from the same direction? Why hadn't the wind stayed north-west instead of shifting north-east? Why could the sea not be calm? To go east, she would have to take down some sail, reef the main. She had watched Neil doing that, and it wasn't easy. For any kind of speed at all on a windward course it was important to winch the sails in tightly. It was quite possible that she did not have enough strength to get their sails set well on a windward course.

She wanted desperately to go for the closest point of land, but the safest course was for San Francisco. Even if the wind shifted back to the north-west, she could handle it without much change in the sails.

She prayed it would not blow harder, because then she would have to reef the mains'l.

If she had to do it, she would. Somehow, she would get him safely to shore, to hospitals and doctors. Oh, if only he would wake up and be all right! She looked at his head closely, without touching. It didn't look serious, just a bump on his head, yet he showed no signs of consciousness. A head injury could be anything from mild concussion to . . . something terrible and permanent.

CHAPTER SIX

SERENA found a timer in the after cabin and used it when she could stay awake no longer. She set it for fifteen minutes, then let her eyes close as she huddled in the cockpit. In little bits and pieces, she caught some sleep. Usually she would jerk awake before the timer went off, her eyes flying to Neil and finding him still there, still unconscious. Then the sails, but they were always the same, too.

Sometime in the middle of the night his lips moved. She groped for his hand inside the sleeping-bag and held it, but he said no words, and his eyelids were still, covering those deep brown eyes she yearned to see again. After a while she decided that she must have imagined the whisper of sound from his lips, perhaps even imagined the movement of those still lips.

She kissed him but he did not feel the caress, and his lips seemed cold. She felt the scratchy abrasion of his fair beard and wondered if it was a good sign that his whiskers still grew even though he was unconscious. Then, finally, she dozed off again, his hand still in hers. She wished she could get him inside, into his bed, but he was too heavy.

What if it rained? She would have to do something then, but she knew there was no way she could get his weight into the cockpit, much less down the stairs into the after cabin. If it did rain, she would have to get a tarpaulin out of the lazaretto and somehow rig it over him.

She tried the radio once more, and again there was
no answer. There was no one to help her, so she had
to do this herself, alone. There were people on shore
who loved him, needed him. His son, his brothers,
his mother. She loved him, too. A new love, but it
was hurting terribly.

By morning, she knew that she would have to reef
the mains'l. She put it off, but the wind strengthened
all through the morning hours. The autopilot began
to wander, and she had trouble keeping on her
course. That was the signal Neil always heeded.
When the steering began to get difficult, it was time
to reduce sail.

It took a long time, and she forced herself to be
careful. She made mistakes, letting the sail down too
far, then having to winch it back up. She pulled as
hard as she could on the winch, but the sail was not
as tight as it had been before. She tied the reefing
ties, but did not take a chance on doing up the ones
that were outboard. Getting rid of the bag in the
bottom of the sail wasn't worth the chance of falling
over. Even with a safety line, leaning outboard would
be risky.

Back in the cockpit she looked at the sail and
decided it was all right. That ripple wouldn't be there
if she'd been able to pull harder on the halyard, and
maybe in a while she would go back and try to get it
tighter, but they were sailing on course, and the
autopilot was behaving itself again.

After dark the wind dropped, but she decided
against taking the reef out. She didn't want to have to
put it in again in the dark. Then, an hour later, the
wind came up in a gusty blow that lasted half the
night, sending *Passagemaker* tearing through the

waves. Thank goodness she had left the reef in! She should have a second reef, too, but the motion was far too wild for her to risk going on deck. In the end she had to turn off the autopilot and steer by hand, keeping an erratic course, everywhere from ninety degrees to two hundred.

She was exhausted by dawn when the wind dropped to fifteen, knots. Her legs were trembling from standing for so many hours while she clung to the wheel. When she could no longer hold the wheel, she put the autopilot back on. Thankfully, it held their course, although the seas were still terribly big.

Neil had moved once in the night, half turning, then falling back, but he did not stir when she called his name. She tried the radio several times again, but there was still no answer, although they were thirty miles closer to land now, angling in towards San Francisco.

She sank down beside him, touching his face and finding it cool, feeling his breath against her fingers. She probed inside the sleeping-bag and his heartbeat was still strong. She hoped he was warm enough. She was shivering herself, even in the cruiser suit. It was tiredness, she supposed, but it felt deadly cold.

When had she eaten? Not since Neil had collapsed, that was certain. She went downstairs. Neil cooked soup on the gimballed gas stove, but she was leery of that with so much motion. She got herself a packet of crackers and some cheese from the refrigerator, added a can of Coke from the cooler and took her crazy picnic up into the cockpit.

She was starving, truly ravenous for the first time since leaving Victoria. She ate it all and drank the

Coke, then fell asleep with her hand holding Neil's, praying for him to wake, to be all right.

Exhausted, she slept on and off through the day, getting up a couple of times to chart her course. Once, she jerked awake, certain she had heard a voice on the radio. She grabbed the microphone and called again and again, but there was nothing.

When the sun went down that night it was unbelievably cold, worse than any night yet. She went forward to her cabin—the first time she had been there in days—and the motion was just as sickening as it had been that first night. She grabbed her sleeping-bag quickly and took it to the cockpit, huddling in the corner, bundled up with the sleeping-bag over her cruiser suit. She set the timer and slept in jerks, her head cradled on the arm that stretched over to hold Neil's hand. She felt very alone.

There was a strangely persistent ache in his head, somewhere behind his eyes. That and the surging sensation of sailing were the only realities for what seemed an endless time.

He thought there was the low, shaken sound of Serena calling his name, begging him to live. Then her voice drifted away and he realised that he was mixed up. Serena was a dream. No, she—was she the dream? Or was she living the dream of an old love? He wasn't sure, but thinking about her hurt somehow, so he let it go, let the dizziness sweep back.

He thought he felt the heat of the sun on his face once, but it was a dark, overcast, moonless night. For a funny moment he wasn't sure where he was, then he realised he was at home, in his own bed, the fan blowing air across his bedding. He should turn it off. It was far too cold, incredibly cold for Mexico.

Soon he would get up and turn it off, although if he waited there would be another of those inevitable power failures and the fan would stop of its own accord. He moved his head, but it was pounding wildly in one of those fierce headaches he used to have as a child.

He let sleep take him again, a dream where his fingers curled around a soft, warm hand . . . Serena . . . No, that was the dream, wasn't it? Sandra. It must be Sandra, although that seemed even less real. He let the confusion go, drifting away again, his fingers curling on hers as he lost consciousness.

In the end he woke slowly, his mind numbed, gradually seeming to clear. It was like a problem in school, the solution coming step by step. The motion, sounds penetrating slowly. Water. The surging, boiling sound. Wind . . . He was sailing. Lying on deck, bundled up somehow. He should get up soon, tend the sail. He must have fallen asleep during his watch, but it was time now to check everything and trim the sail better for this course.

His body did not respond to the instructions of his brain. Soon. Soon he would get up. Serena? His fingers curled, but the hand holding his belonged to the dream. Of course. She was down below, sleeping in his cabin. He liked that. He felt the stiffness of his face as his lips smiled. In a minute he would go down below and watch her sleeping, her dark hair tumbled in wild curls over his pillow, her lips slightly parted, her face smooth and vulnerable and lovely in sleep.

It was a long time since he had thought about a woman the way he thought about Serena, and he was not entirely comfortable with his thoughts. He had been living alone, except for Keith, for so long that he was nervous of letting someone else close enough to affect his life.

After Sandra, there had been that long, lonely emptiness, painfully barren. Then, slowly, he had learned to live again, concentrating on the circumnavigation and on his son, slowly learning joy in being able to reach out and experience the world again. His new freedom would have been terribly lonely if Keith had not been there to share it. He had spent two years doing the things he might have done if it had not been for the early marriage, although it had been long months before he could reach out to a woman again.

Gail had helped, a sensual warmth when he was cold, giving without asking for things he could not feel. No one else had really touched him, until a small, dark woman with curly hair had backed into him at the kick-off party. Serena. Perhaps he was simply lonely, and she had bumped into him just when he needed someone to touch again. San Francisco. Her eyes had promised him San Francisco, and he hoped that would be enough. Each day at sea she seemed to wrap her presence around him so subtly that he began to think sometimes that she was a part of his life, as necessary as breathing was.

He dreamed about waking her from sleep. It was crazy, but that thought haunted him almost as much as the desire to possess her warm body. At night, with the stars overhead, the thought of waking her was with him like a promise.

When it was time, he would go down below, reach out and touch her shoulder lightly and she would wake, her eyes flying open, looking for him in that instant of waking. He loved watching her as she woke, loved climbing into his bed later and feeling her warmth still lingering, breathing in the wonderful scent of her, promising himself that there would be all the time he needed to explore this wonderful woman when they reached San Francisco.

He drifted on the hypnotic motion, hovering on the verge of waking, not able to make himself get up. He must be more tired than he thought, dropping out like this in the middle of his shift. Surprising, because he had been sleeping well ever since Serena had started taking her watches.

He felt a touch, soft against the sleeping-bag, and realised that Serena must have woken and found him out here. Some captain, letting his crew catch him sleeping on watch! Funny, he couldn't remember getting the sleeping-bag out.

Her hand slid though the bag, found his. He caught her fingers and held them. 'How are you feeling?' he asked her, his voice coming strangely weak and hoarse, as if he were the weak one instead of her.

'Neil?' She sounded trembly, in the grip of emotion too strong. 'Neil? Are you awake?' He tried to laugh, but his head hurt terribly and the chuckle would not escape his throat. Heavens, it was dark! He could not see her at all. There was just her voice and the trembling, warm touch of her hand on his. 'Neil, are you all right?'

He concentrated, trying to catch the train of his thought again. 'The patch will be wearing off by now,' he managed finally. 'Are you feeling seasick?'

Patch? She shook her head, confused. He was watching her, but even in faint moonlight she felt there was no awareness in his eyes. As if he were still not truly awake. Of course he would be confused. Concussion.

'You were knocked out,' she said, then realised what he had been talking about. 'I took the patch off,' she told him, her fingers straying to the faintly itchy spot behind her ear. 'I think I'm used to the motion now. I'm not sick at all.' There had been that awful wave of nausea when she had gone forward for the sleeping-bag, but there was no need to mention that. 'Neil, are you all right?' He was awake, but not moving. She was suddenly frightened that there was more damage than just the bump. What if he was paralysed? He did not answer and she said urgently, 'Neil, can you move?'

'Of course,' he whispered. 'Just kind of tired.' He shifted then and she saw his leg move, his hip thrust out as he turned towards her slightly, then fell back. 'Headache,' he managed then. 'Haven't had one in years. I'll get up in a second.'

Ice, she thought. There was ice in the freezer. She could put some in a towel and put it on that lump on his head. She bit her lip, hesitating. Cold, and he might be suffering from shock already. It would be better if she could get him inside first, tucked warmly into his berth.

'Neil, can you get up?' His eyes closed and she said urgently, 'Neil, please wake up! I want you to get up, to get into your bed.'

He was gone again. She felt his fingers slack on hers. His lips moved and she had to bend down to catch his question. 'Is it your watch now, Serena?'

'Yes,' she whispered, holding his fingers tightly. She didn't care about watches if he was all right. 'It's my watch.'

He nodded slightly, his head hardly moving, whispered, 'Then I'll just sleep here a bit, I think. Wake me up when it's my turn.'

It was a good sign, wasn't it? He had woken, so he was not in some kind of deadly coma. She had seen his leg move, felt his fingers. There couldn't be anything broken, or he would have told her, wouldn't he? Headache, he had said, and that was no wonder! Maybe he'd be a day or two getting back to normal. That was OK. She could handle the boat somehow. She would get them into San Francisco and there would be a doctor who would say it was OK, that it was only a bump and what was the fuss?

She smiled over that. Medical things were usually that way. You went for a terrible pain and learned that it was indigestion. It hadn't been that way for Terry. He'd had those funny sensations, then he had fallen one day and it hadn't been a false alarm at all but a deadly disease that had taken him away from her. But it wouldn't be like that again. Neil was too strong. He'd be fine.

She felt vitally awake, ready for anything. She went down below and put a kettle on the gas range, tightening the sea rail to be sure it didn't move. Then she checked Neil again, but he was sleeping and seemed to be comfortable. Next time he woke, she would make sure to get him properly into bed; meanwhile, she would look after things. She smiled again, deciding that he would be surprised at how well she was coping.

She put away the broken tackle and found fresh sheets for his bed. Then she went to the boiling kettle and managed to do the dishes, which was quite an accomplishment in the middle of a heaving sea. She was pleased with herself. She would make a real sailor yet! She got everything put away, the dishes and the cloth and the towel, but she would have forgotten to close the drain valve to the sink if the boat hadn't bounced down on a big wave that made a geyser of water shoot up through the drain. She fumbled in the cupboard then and got the valve closed. Then she cleaned up the water so he wouldn't know. Well, perhaps she'd tell him about it when he woke up. He would laugh, and it would be nice to hear his low chuckle again.

She didn't bother to call on the radio again. There was no longer an emergency. He was getting better. He didn't need rescuing, and she could handle the boat if the weather didn't do anything too drastic. Of course, he should see a doctor, but he would be up tomorrow and he would want to get anchored in San Francisco first. San Francisco was getting a lot closer.

He slept all through the day, waking briefly once and asking for water. She brought him a cup and he spilled some, but he drank deeply and then slept again. He turned on his side sometime in the afternoon and seemed to be sleeping very naturally. She wished she had managed to get him inside, but other than that everything was all right.

She got the stays'l up again as the wind lightened, and even ventured out to take the reef out of the main. The seas were smaller now and she got a good grip on the halyard and pulled the main up quite respectably tight.

According to her calculations, if they kept on at six knots, they would be in San Francisco tomorrow afternoon. After dark the wind dropped still more and she decided it was time to put up the big jib sail. They hadn't flown that since Jaun de Fuca Strait, but now was time again. She got it set and *Passagemaker* picked up a knot in speed.

She saw a blip on the radar that must be another boat. It passed by, heading north, and never came close enough for her to see what it was. An hour later, she saw another blip. They were getting close to the shipping lanes. Luckily she wasn't really tired any more. She would be later, of course, but maybe Neil would be awake then and he could watch while she caught a bit of sleep.

She would never have believed she could do all this alone, tending the boat and the man, sailing alone with no land, no sign of life anywhere. It was amazing what a person could do when it was necessary, but she wished she had been more use to him earlier in the voyage.

The seas continued to subside through the early part of the night, but the wind held at about ten knots and they were moving very pleasantly through the water. She could see lights sometimes now, other boats, some of them big.

'Hello, love.'

She jumped, then swung to look at him. His voice was very low, right beside her, marvellously awake and alive.

'Hi,' she whispered, joy piercing her heart. It was wonderful! The sky and the stars and the lovely soft swell lifting the boat from time to time, And Neil, close by her, alive.

'I missed you holding my hand,' he said, his voice odd. She pushed back the sleeping-bag and his hand found hers. He was strangely passive.

'I've been worried about you getting cold. Are

you really conscious now? Can you get up? I want to get you down to your bunk.' She wished she could see him a little better, but there was no moon tonight, only the stars. She had turned out the light in the after cabin earlier because the battery voltage was getting low. Now there was only the green glow of the radar and the Loran, and a million tiny stars.

She thought she saw his eyes open, then close again. 'Neil, you're not hurt, are you? No broken bones? I tried to check, and I couldn't find anything wrong except the bump on your head. That's why you've got the headache.' His hand left hers, touched his head gingerly. 'Does it still hurt?' She was starting to feel nervous. It was unlike him to lie there passively while she looked after everything. He should be up, looking at the water, the sails, adjusting something that she had not realised needed changing.

'The head? It's a bit better,' he said finally. 'I don't want to move yet. I'm comfortable here. What —what happened, Serena?' She could hear the disorientation in his voice. 'I remember going up to release the preventer for the mains'l, then nothing.'

'The tackle broke. Something hit you in the head, knocked you out. I think it was the metal piece on the bottom of the tackle. It's been—you've been unconscious for almost two days.' He said nothing and for a long moment she thought he was sleeping again. Then he stirred and she said, 'I called on the radio. I tried and tried, but we must have been too far out. I could call now. We're closer, and I think——'

'No!' She could feel the tension in him, but did not understand it. He said tightly, 'I don't want

stretchers and doctors and——' He was breathing too
quickly, then he seemed suddenly too still.

'Neil?' She found his other hand, held them both in
hers. She didn't understand, but she had to reassure
him. It frightened her that he held her hand so
tightly. 'It's all right. I won't call on the radio if you
don't want me to.'

'You might,' he sounded odd, almost frightened, 'if
I fall asleep again, and you decide I'd be better off
in a hospital. Then you might.' He was afraid, for
some reason, of losing control.

'What's wrong, Neil?' Something was. She should
have known. All these hours and he hadn't got
up.

'Are there many stars tonight?' He shifted,
propping himself up on one elbow, leaning towards
her, still holding her left hand with his.

'Millions. Don't change the subject, please, Neil.
What's wrong?'

His fingers tightened on hers. 'Where are we?'

'Do you want the longitude and latitude?' she
snapped, worried. 'We'll be in San Francisco tomorrow afternoon. If you need to know exactly, I'll go
look at the Loran.'

She gulped, and he must have seen or heard
because he caught her face between his hands and
brought it close to his. His lips brushed hers, then
firmed and she was in his arms, trembling, then
curving close to him, oblivious of even the metal
edge of the winch between them. It was a harsh
kiss and she sensed some need in it beyond her
understanding. Possession without desire, his lips
hard and demanding, hers giving. Then it was over
and she was breathless against him, her head turned
into the curve of his shoulder as she burrowed in

his arms. His hands smoothed the windblown chaos of her hair, taming it, his fingers threading through it.

'I love the feel of your hair, Serena.' His voice was still strained, then he asked, 'If I can't help you, can you bring the boat into San Francisco on your own?'

She swallowed. 'Neil, what's wrong? Is it your legs?'

'No. My head.' His fingers probed the back of her head. She felt a stiffness in him, as if he were about to push her away, yet he held her close. 'I'm going to have to get medical attention, but I'd very much like to do it under my own steam.' He took a deep breath, then admitted unwillingly, 'I need a little time first. I—you won't call on the radio?'

'Only if you're unconscious,' she promised him. 'I—I believe that a person should have the right to make their own decisions, even if they're sick.'

'Thank you.' He took a deep breath. She could feel some of the tension flowing out of him. 'I'm sorry I left you alone at sea, Serena,' he said softly. 'I'm sorry I got you into this.'

'It's all right.' She laughed softly and said, 'I've learned quite a bit about sailing. You'd be amazed at what I can do. I reefed the main and took the reef back out later. I put the jib up. We're on a course right for San Francisco.'

'And everything's fine?'

'Yes.' She reached up and found the bristly roughness of his cheek. 'I can get us into harbour, I think. I was studying the chart this afternoon, and it's pretty plain where to go. I don't know what to do once we're in the harbour, though, but if you tell me, I can do it.'

He nodded, and she loved the feel of his chin rough against her hair. 'Iron lady,' he said, an odd note in his voice. 'Who would have thought you had it in you?' He shuddered then and said, 'Thank heaven you do.'

She tipped her head back and could see him worrying his lip with his teeth. He wasn't looking at her, but somewhere over her head, then his arms tensed around her before he dropped them away. 'You'll have to do it, Serena. I can't see.' When she was silent he said harshly, 'Do you understand? That blow must have done something, somehow blinded me.'

'You tricked me,' she accused shakily, her fingers finding his face, touching as if touch were words. 'You made me agree not to call on the radio before you told me——'

'We're even, then, aren't we?' His voice was strained. 'You got me to take you on as crew, pretending you'd done this all before.'

'No, I—you were the one who was determined to have me as crew! You—I tried to say no, but you were——' She had *wanted* to go. Her anger collapsed. She touched his cheek and said shakily, 'I'm sorry. I don't mean to be shouting at you, but—Neil, if your eyes——Shouldn't you get to a hospital as soon as you can? Please.'

He was silent for a long time. He had a pretty good idea of how it would be once he got to a hospital. Doctors. Possibly surgery or, even worse, some white-suited fool telling him that was it, he would never see again. One crazy second on the deck of a boat at sea, then nothing but blackness.

He wanted to put it off, to hang on to Serena and these last few hours at sea, but he couldn't lean on her, cling to her as if he were a weak thing.

'Please,' she whispered, those cool fingers stroking his cheek. 'Time might make a difference, darling. What if——You should get to a hospital as soon as you can. Please, Neil.'

She should have help. She had managed these last two days alone, but how could he ask her to do more than she had already done? One call and there would be the coastguard to take the responsibility from her.

'All right,' he managed. 'Call for help.'

CHAPTER SEVEN

THEY decided eventually that the radio must be broken. The receiver was OK, but no matter how many times she keyed the microphone and called for help, there was no answer. Eventually, Serena gave up trying, conceding that he was right. There was no point.

Neil insisted on taking his turn while she got some sleep, claiming that he was perfectly well except for the inconvenience of not being able to see. She would have preferred to see him sleeping, but he refused. She agreed finally, mainly because he seemed so worried about her being left alone on watch. He got her to bring his cruiser suit and he put it on, then he told her how to set the intrusion alarm on the radar so that it would sound a beep if any boat came within two miles of them. He insisted that he would be able to tell by the sound if the sails needed tending and he would wake her.

She was terrified that he would try to tend the sails while she slept. She kept jerking awake, her eyes flying to the little window for a sign that he was there, in the cockpit still. In fact, while she slept, he used the control lines in the cockpit to bring both the main and jib in tighter, picking up their speed in the ever-decreasing wind.

Dawn was lightening the sky when he woke her. By his calculations he thought they should be forty miles from San Francisco. He was close. She plotted their position and found they were thirty-eight miles from the Golden Gate Bridge. He went to bed then, finally. She hoped he slept.

She altered course as Neil had suggested, turning to approach the port by the north shipping lane. The wind lightened through the morning. For the first time it seemed warm. She took off her cruiser suit.

She was keeping the radar on, even though she could see land. She had been afraid that the batteries would go completely dead, but the low battery problem was solved now. While she had slept, Neil had gone down below and switched batteries. The voltage was now back up to over twelve volts. She had not known there was more than one battery, and had no idea how he had managed to change them over without seeing. She was relieved about the batteries, but frightened because he was so determined to try to tend sails and fumble around for battery switches without being able to see. What if he did something dangerous, was too determined to look after things himself to wake her when he needed her?

During the morning she fussed a little over the set of the sails, pulling them in slightly to compensate for the change in wind. Then she went back into the after cabin and found Neil awake.

'Hello,' she said, sitting down beside him, her hand touching his fleetingly. She usually touched him when they were close, feeling instinctively that he needed the contact. 'How do you feel?'

He smiled, but she could see the lines of tension on his forehead. 'OK except for the headache, but it's getting better.' His fingers curled around her wrist. 'We're almost there?'

She nodded, realised he could not see and said,

'A couple of hours. I passed Point Reyes a while back. I think I'd better start the engine soon. The wind keeps dropping.' She wanted to touch his hair, to comb it with her fingers and smooth the lines of worry on his forehead.

'You'll get wind again when you get near the bridge, but I'll get the sails down before you go under the bridge. It'll be easier for you if you're running by the engine. Any boats around right now?'

He would get the sails down? She hesitated to argue. He was sensitive about his helplessness, although he pretended not to be. She concentrated on his question. Other boats. She glanced at the radar and saw the curve of the bays outside the Golden Gate Bridge, a green splatter that was the bridge itself. There was a boat four miles away, but she had already ascertained that it was moving west, not on a collision course with *Passagemaker*. 'No,' she said. 'There's nothing.'

He was staring up at her. It was hard to believe that he could not see. She felt her breath leave her lungs, her heart fluttering with a kind of delicious panic. She knew what was coming before his hands moved, then she felt him drawing her down gently towards him.

She could easily have escaped his touch. If she had stiffened or drawn back, his fingers would have slipped free and the contact would have been broken. She swallowed and tensed in the instant before she lost her balance.

He stilled, then said awkwardly, 'I can't see you, Serena. It would be easier if I could see your eyes and know what you're thinking.'

She didn't even think of trying to hide her feelings from him. 'Sometimes,' she said tremulously, 'I felt

as if you were looking right through me. I——' She
licked her lips to drive away the dryness, and she
tried to laugh but it failed. 'You're not going to
believe this, Neil, but I get a bit nervous when—it's
been a long time since . . .'

His hands firmed suddenly, drawing her down on
to him. Then he shifted and she was settled into the
curve of his arm, his hand cupping her shoulder,
caressing through her sweater, and his head was
dropping down, his lips finding hers with a sureness
that did not need sight.

'You smell nice,' he said huskily as his lips explored
hers slowly. 'What scent is it?'

'Krystle,' she managed raggedly. His tongue traced
the shape of her lips, then he explored the fullness of
her cheek, the soft trembling of her eyelids under his
kiss. His fingers on her shoulder urged her closer as
he explored her face with his mouth, and she was a
trembling softness, clinging to him, her arms
somehow wrapped around his shoulders, holding
her against the sweeping dizziness that his other
hand brought, the fingers resting almost innocently
against the softness of her midriff.

'What are you wearing?' Her lips had opened and
his had found them, his warm, moist tongue
exploring the dark mystery of her mouth. His hand
slipped over the sweater, exploring, finding the
thrust of her hip. 'Tell me,' he urged huskily.

'A sweater.' His mouth probed down to the
sensitive skin under her jaw. 'Red sweater,' she
gasped as his fingers slipped under it at her waist,
caressing her shuddering flesh with the most fleeting
of warm, sensuous touches.

'The one with the buttons?' His hand left her
midriff, touched where the butons were open at her

neck, stroked the bare exposed triangle of skin below her throat. 'You wore it the first day you were on the boat?'

'Yes.' Oh, she was aching! His touch was so soft, so achingly slow, and she was burning up with need. His voice seemed to tease, to caress, to send the fire licking along her veins. Did he mean to be doing this? Could he feel her going wild with his slow, husky voice caressing her? She could not stop the restless, sensuous movement of her body against his.

'That sweater makes me wild,' he told her huskily. 'Just one more button.' His fingers fumbled and the sweater was open one more button, the lace of her brassiere showing, if only he could see. His touch followed the edges of the neckline, finding the soft swelling above her bra. 'I wanted to do that all day when you were wearing this.'

He must feel her heart thundering. Her breath was ragged, his fingers lifting with the uneven movement of her lungs. She didn't know when, but her eyes had closed and there was only the dizzy darkness and Neil.

'Please,' she whispered, begging him for she knew not what.

'It's all right,' his voice promised softly, and the buttons were all undone, his hand exploring the aching arousal of her breasts through the lace as his lips found the soft, trembling hollow of her throat. 'You're beautiful,' he groaned against the cleavage exposed above her bra, and she shuddered, forgetting that he could not see her until he said raggedly, 'What colour is this?' his fingers somehow finding the catch that would release her aching flesh to his touch.

'Red.' She swallowed, twisted against him and

felt his leg going over hers, pinning her down with a wonderful heaviness that brought a formless sound to her throat.

'Red,' he said raggedly. 'Matches the sweater.' Then he growled low against the suddenly free curves of her breasts, his hand cupping the warmth for his lips to find.

She started to laugh at the low, sensuous growl, then she gasped as his lips found the engorged peak of her nipple, and there was the spinning, starlit explosion of feeling, a formless need that flowed everywhere, then focused sharply in a thick, heavy heartbeat that shook the very centre of her womanhood.

'Please,' she whispered, and he could have no doubt of her meaning, her heated female curves twisting against him. She could feel his response, hard against her, then he shifted and she was lying on top of him, his hands at her waist, pushing down the soft fabric of her jogging pants. She wriggled free of the fabric, helping him, needing the feel of his rigid maleness against her.

Then there was only Neil, warm flesh against her softness, heated hardness pressing into her, nothing between them but the flimsy barrier of her panties and his brief jockey shorts.

'Kiss me, darling,' he groaned, and her lips opened, her tongue meeting his, their mouths together plundering a deep, passionate need, symbolic of that other dark invasion that their bodies strained for.

His hands slipped down over her body, moulding her against him, slipping under the panties and cupping the firm roundness of her buttocks, holding her hard against him for an earthshaking moment.

'Neil——'

'Serena—oh, lord!' His hands held her rigidly as he gasped, 'Be very still for a moment. Please, darling!' Then he was turning, her body sliding from his, lying against the mattress as he said softly, 'There isn't another woman like you in the world. Did you know that?'

She shook her head silently, reaching for him, begging without words for his touch on her again. A shudder went through him, then he bent to her, his lips tender against hers as he whispered raggedly, 'I want you very much, lovely Serena, but there's no way I can protect you if I take you.' His lips silenced whatever word she might have said as his hands found the swelling of her breasts and his thumbs softly rubbed the rigid peaks.

What was he doing? Was he pushing her away, or not? His words seemed to say one thing and his touch another. She shuddered, her arms reaching for him, her lips parting against his shoulder as his head bent lower.

'Neil, I don't—if——'

His hands were touching, his lips finding their way down to the softness of her breasts. It felt so good, so wonderfully right to have his tongue touching there, his ragged groan against her. Then his hand pushed down the lace barrier of her panties and he touched her very softly, turning her to a shuddering need.

'Let me make love to you like this,' he whispered, touching her, kissing her, sending the world away into a spinning vortex of passion.

Later he held her close against him, kissing her closed eyelids, smoothing her damp curls away from her forehead.

'Neil, you—what about you? I——'

'The headache helps,' he said, a wry smile in his voice. He was holding her closely and she could not see his face. 'Thank you, Serena,' he said finally, quietly. 'Thank you for giving yourself to me.'

'But——' She struggled up, leaning on her elbow, trying to see what was in his face. She felt a sudden, hot self-consciousness. He had not taken her in the conventional sense, but she felt just as vulnerable as if he had, perhaps more so. She remembered his touch and her wild need, and knew that he could have little doubt of her feelings. She knew, too, that he was more comfortable with her needs than with his own.

I love you. The words surged up in her mind, but she was silent. As his silence stretched, she became uncomfortably aware of her naked body in his arms, of her vulnerability and his tension. 'I'd better see where we are,' she said stiffly. Could a man make love, so *lovingly*, without loving?

Her eyes went to the radar screen. There were no immediate dangers, but she stumbled away from him, pulling on her clothes. Had she thought that she could share herself with him for a while and then walk away? It was not true. It mattered terribly.

Why did he not say anything?

She went up above and followed the instructions he gave her for starting the engine. Behind her, she was aware of him moving, dressing, and she did not look, did not even want to look. She hugged herself and stared ahead at the land that seemed to be disappearing into a thickening fog. She tried to gather some kind of emotional barrier around herself.

Neil dressed slowly, forcing himself to patience with his fumbling fingers. He wished painfully that he had controlled his selfish need to have her in his arms, to feel the soft trembling of her woman's warmth. He had pulled her down into his arms, needing desperately to touch, to know that he could make her need him.

Childish selfishness, grabbing for what he wanted, using her warmth to shield him from his own fears. He had never before woken in the dark, unable to turn on the lights, not knowing if there would ever be light again. He was terrified of walking into a hospital and being told that whatever had happened inside his head was forever. But, damn it, that was no excuse for seducing Serena, then lying silent while he could feel her need for words. What words had she wanted him to say? Love? Commitment? What could a blind man promise, anyway?

The headache was worse. That was a bad sign. He could feel the ominous pressure in his skull, yet held back from the horrible drama of telling Serena to get out flares, to signal for help. Ambulances. Doctors. He had always felt impatient with people who put off going to the doctor because they were afraid to learn an unpleasant truth—yet now the irrational child in him wanted to escape the inevitable by procrastination.

His arms wanted to pull her back, but how could he know what he was reaching for? For Serena? Or simply for someone, anyone, to shield him from his own fears? The rational part of him was afraid to reach for her, to respond to the warm caring in her voice, her touch. She had lived with an invalid husband, caring for him, loving him. She was stronger than he had realised, and her very strength frightened him. Perhaps it was his helplessness, his blindness, that attracted her. He hated that thought. It brought a fantasy of himself, helpless forever, dependent on her, clinging and needing.

He had to keep control of what was happening to him, especially inside his mind. He concentrated on the details, getting dressed in the dark, going outside and feeling the sun on his head without seeing light.

He could remember the passage under the Golden Gate Bridge, amazingly could even remember how many buoys there were in that narrow passage north of the shipping lane. He guided her through, his memories matching what she saw on the chart. As usual, the bridge was shrouded in fog and she could not see, but it did not matter. There were his memories, the chart, the radar picture for her eyes.

He heard the awe in her voice as they passed under that beautiful, fog-shrouded bridge. Then, once inside, her relief. 'The fog's lifting, Neil!'

He shared her worry as she tried to pick out the landmarks in his mind. 'Just follow the shore to the left. We'll anchor in Richardson Bay instead of going into San Francisco itself.' Was his memory reliable? How many times had he piloted this boat along this shore? Four, perhaps five. Was there a hazard he could not remember? 'Stay a hundred yards offshore and go until you see a building on a point on pilings. Then——' Did she know how far a hundred yards was? She had become a very competent sailor at sea, but this was the coast, with rocks and shallows and——'

'There it is! Neil, the building's there, over the water! It's all windows, looks like a restaurant or something. Is that it?'

'That's it.' His hand found hers, a touch that seemed to reassure her.

'Neil, dar . . . there's another boat just ahead. We'll be passing him.' He thought her heard her swallow, then she said tensely, 'I'll go closer and shout over. He can call on his radio and——'

'No!' Not yet! He wasn't ready yet, must have more time. It was ridiculously important that he walk into the hospital on his own feet, in his own time. Not rational, but he had a terrible conviction that if he gave up control of this day he would never see again. 'We'll anchor. There's no need for——Just head for that building, then follow the markers. Keep the red markers on your right.'

She was standing very close to him, her hands on the wheel. They were not touching, yet he could feel the tension as her will fought his. He was half afraid that she could feel his tension and his fear. He felt the wind on his face and his mind presented a picture of Serena, her eyes narrowed against the sun, her copper-highlighted curls tumbling wonderfully in the breeze. What would it be like to live with a woman like her—strong and resilient?

He pushed the temptation to weakness aside, groped desperately for strength. 'Serena, an hour isn't going to make any difference. My headache's gone.' The pain surged up to punish him for that lie, but he managed, 'Let's just anchor.'

He didn't know what made her give way, whether she believed his lie about the headache or not. But she followed the channel in, and he concealed his relief when she said that the anchorage was not too badly crowded.

'All right,' he said. 'Go in slowly to the centre of the largest area between the boats. Very slowly.

I'll go forward and get the anchor ready, then just call out to me when we're in the centre and I'll let her go.'

'Neil, I can do it. I—'

'No!' He had a horrible fantasy of her fumbling that chain in her inexperience, getting a finger or a leg caught as the heavy, dangerous chain surged out over the bow roller. 'Just do it the way I said!'

He untied the anchor first, the big Bruce that he used as a storm anchor. Its extra holding area should make up for the fact that he could not see to do a proper job of setting it. He checked with his hands that there was nothing in the way for the chain to catch. Then he took the pipe and put it over the lever point, ready for her call. He could feel the engine vibration changing as she backed off on the throttle. He cranked the lever just as she called 'Now!'

He couldn't see the markers on the chain, but was pretty sure that he had about a hundred and fifty feet out when he put the brake on for the last time. He felt the boat lurch as the rode came tight, then start to swing. The anchor was well set.

'OK!' His head pulsed painfully as he shouted, 'Kill the engine!' He reached and caught hold of the stays'l boom, fighting dizziness.

Silence. He was still, listening to the soft sounds of the vessel lying in the water, the more distant blare of a car horn on shore. He could hear Serena as she moved softly along the deck. She was wearing running shoes and they squeaked faintly on the teak. He remembered the one time he had taken Sandra out sailing, and he realised more strongly than ever how different the two women were.

'Customs next,' he told her, the words seeming to fade away from him. The moment of truth was getting horribly closer. Customs, then it would have to be the hospital. He made his voice casual, said, 'We have to report in to Customs before we do anything else.'

'No!' Her hands gripped his arms, the first time she had touched him since she left his arms that morning. 'No more delays, Neil!'

He knew that he could not fight her any longer. He felt himself reel, the world losing equilibrium. He thought her arms went around him, holding him, and he knew there wasn't much time. He managed, 'Serena, don't tell my family.'

Then everything went black.

CHAPTER EIGHT

THE PEOPLE in the boat nearest *Passagemaker* heard the first time she shouted. Coastguard. Stretcher. Paramedics. Neil looked so terribly pale under that tan. A quick, wild ride to the hospital, sirens going. He didn't move at all. The noise and the terror was building inside Serena. He was going to die, and she would be alone forever because there would never be another man who could touch her soul as he did. Then the waiting, the horrible time in hospital chairs, white-uniformed people looking at her with that cold sympathy, but not telling her anything.

Terry. Poor Terry, his life slipping away.

The doctor frowning at her, telling her almost nothing. 'We're waiting for the results of the X-ray. We're going to need his next of kin for their consent.'

'I'll call his brother.'

'Don't tell my family,' he had said. But that was wrong. The people who loved him had a right to know he was in danger. His brother. His son.

She fumbled her way through the telephone's information services. Area code for San Diego, Information. 'Turner, please.' There were many Turners, but the name Zeb was less common and she got the number. Then the man.

'Hello, I—I'm Serena Jones. I was crewing for your brother Neil on——'

'What's happened to Neil?' He sounded wonderfully strong and competent. And quick. He listened to her stumbling, frightened half-explanation, didn't ask useless questions, simply said, 'I'll fly my own plane up. Tell the doctor I'll be there in three hours at the most. Meanwhile, Serena, could I get you to do a few things?'

'Yes?'

Anything that took her attention away from that hospital corridor seemed like too much, but he instructed her, 'Call Customs and report the boat's entry into the country, report the emergency. Maybe the coastguard did that, but you should also to explain why you've not followed proper entry procedure. Then make me a reservation at a hotel near the hospital. Reserve two rooms. Then call the marinas and yacht clubs and see if you can arrange berthage for *Passagemaker*.'

There was only the waiting. Zeb's list of tasks kept her busy, and she half suspected he had given her so many time-consuming tasks for that reason. No one would tell her anything about Neil. She wished she had lied, told them she was a wife or fiancée or something that would mean she could have access to that room where they had him. They should let her in, let her touch his hand, talk to him. What if he woke up in the dark? She wanted to be there. She knew he was afraid. He had pretended not to be, but the worry was there in the lines around his sightless eyes. She wished he had shared it with her, because sharing might have made it easier for him, and would surely have made it easier for her.

It was dark outside now. Would they do anything about Neil in the night? What were they doing? What had the X-rays shown? Why would no one tell her anything? She tried to read a magazine, but the words stumbled across her brain like hieroglyphic symbols. She got a cup of coffee from a machine in the corridor, but it tasted terrible. She drank it anyway.

How many times in her life would this happen to her? Sitting in a hospital, worrying, not knowing. She mustn't let herself think that it would not be all right. Maybe her thoughts mattered, affected the outcome somehow. It could be fine, Neil might be himself again after some surgical magic. Yet his eyes had been affected, and he had lost consciousness again, and things going wrong inside a person's head could be so terribly final. He might die.

She kept looking at her watch. It was ten-thirty by the time the elevator doors slid open and the man and boy stepped out. The man was taller than Neil, his hair medium brown, his body lean with the kind of hardness that came from swimming and tennis, not from hard work outdoors. The boy was almost as tall, but thin, as if he had just shot up six inches and his body was desperately trying to cope with the wild increase in height. He was very fair, his hair blond with the same unruly determination as Neil's.

The man headed straight for her, the boy slightly behind. 'Serena?' His voice had the calm strength of a man accustomed to taking charge. Another Turner man. 'I'm Zeb. How is he?'

'The nurse says there's no change. They won't let me see him.' She managed to keep her voice from breaking, but she had a terrible temptation to collapse, to cry and beg this man to make things right for Neil.

'I'll see what I can find out.' He touched her hand fleetingly, reassuringly. He sounded as if he could fix anything. That was ridiculous, because Neil needed doctors' magic, but he was that kind of man. He glanced at the boy, said, 'Keith, stay here with Serena.'

'But——' The boy swallowed. Serena could see him marshalling arguments against being confined to the waiting-room. She thought he was at the stage where he argued a lot.

Zeb said gently, 'Keith, if your dad regains consciousness, they might let you in to see him. So stay here while I go and try to round up the doctor.'

'OK,' he agreed, collapsing his length into the chair beside Serena. When they were alone, Serena asked, 'Can I get you a Coke?' He shook his head and she offered, 'Or a coffee?'

'No.' He did not look at her, but at the floor, as if the pattern of dark and light tiles was important to his survival. She wanted to reassure him somehow, but there was nothing she could say that would be both reassuring and true.

The wail of an ambulance siren penetrated the corridor, seeming to wake Keith from his trance. 'Is my dad going to die?' His voice was tight, his eyes seeming to accuse her.

'I don't know,' she whispered. 'I hope not.' She wished that she had told Neil she loved him. The words had been there, on her lips, but she had pushed them back, afraid to expose herself to hurt.

Keith's teeth gnawed at his upper lip. He lifted thin fingers and brushed the hair back from his forehead. His eyes were a deep blue, not his father's dark brown, and he was suffering from the teenager's typical inability to sit still. She wondered if Sandra had had blue eyes, and supposed that she must have.

'Are you and my father——' He flushed and his eyes dropped away from hers. His feet moved restlessly on the floor. 'Are you his woman?'

'No, I—I'm his crew.' The boy was hunched over, not looking at her, a tension in him as if rejecting her explanation. She had a vision of Neil leaning over her, his hand caressing her breast, and it was so vivid that she could feel herself flushing. She said, 'I met him in Victoria. He asked me to crew for him when you couldn't come.'

'Oh.' He twitched in the seat, jerked his head to throw a lock of hair back. 'I—ah—we had a fight.'

She saw him blinking and knew that he would hate himself if he cried in front of her. 'Bad fight?' she asked, wanting to take him in her arms and knowing she must not.

'Yeah.' He shifted his legs and sank lower into the chair, his legs stretching out into the room awkwardly. 'He wouldn't let me go on this trip to Mexico City.' He shifted, said sulkily, 'I'm sixteen. He can't keep me locked up forever, can he? I told him I wanted to go to a private school, or to Uncle Zeb, but no matter what, I didn't want to live with him any more.' She saw the convulsive movement of his throat. 'We did a lot of shouting.'

She touched his arm and he did not jerk away, although she felt him tense for a moment, then relax. He would not look at her. She tried to remember what Neil had said about his problems with Keith. 'He said he thought it would be best for you to go to a regular school now, but that he would miss you a lot. He was thinking about leaving Mexico, coming up here for you.'

'He shouldn't do that!' Keith was startled, upset. 'He likes it there, and it's a super place! The swimming's great, you know. The marina is getting pretty big, and he's talking about building boats down there.' He was talking quickly, piling details into the conversation as if to win some point. 'He's been training José and Carlos and—he shouldn't leave.' He frowned and gulped, said, 'Especially not just for me. Did he really say that?'

She looked at his bent head and wished she could take him in her arms. 'Your dad can see you're growing up. He's having a little trouble letting go, but he wants to do what's best for you. He loves you. If you don't think he should leave Mexico, why don't you tell him that?'

He pulled away, abruptly self-conscious. 'Are you gonna marry my dad?'

She shook her head. It was too soon. She was too uncertain of Neil's feelings. She suppressed a sudden yearning for children, a shared home. Neil was attracted to her, but that was a long way from a lifetime commitment. A million miles away. The only commitment he had made was a half-promise of a week in San Francisco. One week.

'You figure it's none of my business?' Keith's voice had risen, taken on a surly tone. She thought about the teenage boys she taught, and recognised the quick defensiveness concealed by anger.

'I don't know how to answer you, Keith. Your dad—Neil and I haven't—we haven't even talked about love, much less marriage.'

'Oh.' He stared at her, then seemed embarrassed at his own scrutiny. He looked down the hallway at the coffee machine. 'D'ya want a cup of coffee?'

'Sure. Thanks.' It was terrible coffee. She tried to look as if she was enjoying it, then Zeb came and she put the Styrofoam cup down on a table and conveniently forgot to finish it.

'I talked to the doctor and had a look at the X-rays.' She could see Neil in him as he stood there, the concern suppressed in his eyes, but there. These men must have learned early to hide their emotions, although Zeb seemed to have learned it better than his brother. 'The surgeon insists there's nothing that can't be easily repaired. They're going to operate tonight.'

They all turned to the approaching nurse, waiting tensely for what she might say. Serena hated this constant dread, the feeling that everyone was hiding unpleasant truths from her.

'Mr Turner, the doctor says the family can see your brother for a moment before they prepare him for surgery, as long as you're careful not to disturb him.'

Family. She wasn't family, but she wanted terribly to see him. She glanced up at Zeb and he nodded, taking her arm as if she belonged, too. 'Come on, Keith. Let's go see your dad.'

Keith walked ahead of them and she had a moment to whisper to Zeb, 'What about his eyes?'

'I don't know. The surgeon is hoping that it's simply a problem caused by pressure on the optic nerve, that after surgery and when the inflammation has subsided it'll be all right.'

Had she hurt him when she had dragged him back along the deck? She forgot about the others—Zeb and Keith. She moved slowly, very quietly to the bed. She touched Neil's hand. *Please*, she found herself praying, but she could not even form words, only an aching prayer.

I love you. Why hadn't she told him that? What if there was never a chance again?

She became aware of someone touching her, turned and saw Zeb beside her, but he was blurred with her tears. Damn! How could she be so powerless? Why wasn't there something she could do about this?

Her eyes sought Keith and found him standing with his back against the window, his face set hard to conceal his emotions. She pulled away from Zeb and went to the boy, but he turned his face away from her.

'You'll have to leave now,' said the nurse, too soon, and they left the room together, walking out in single file like three people numbed.

They waited. Zeb tried to keep them occupied, asking Serena questions about how she had met Neil, about the voyage, the accident, trying to get Keith to talk about the marina in Mexico. Serena tried to respond, but her mind wouldn't stay on her words. Keith didn't even try to answer. Finally Zeb gave up, falling silent himself.

When Keith disappeared to go to the toilet, Zeb said, 'He's going through problems with his dad. They've been fighting about everything, and I don't think either one of them knows how to stop.'

She remembered how Neil's eyes had clouded as he had talked about his son, and knew that Zeb was right. 'What about you?' she asked, putting together the bits of knowledge she had about Zeb Turner. 'Are you the fixer? Everyone in the family turns to you in trouble, don't they?'

'I guess.' He smiled a little, admitted, 'I think it's the heritage my dad left me. I have a family full of people who have leaned on me all my adult life. My brother Barry, his ex-wife, my mother.' He smiled wryly. 'Not Neil, though. Neil likes doing things his own way. Trying to interfere in his life has got me into one or two of the hottest battles of my life. When he's had trouble, he's always been determined to stand alone.'

His eyes went to the corridor, the closed doors that hid the surgery from them. 'I can't get my mind to accept the idea of him helpless. He must hate it.'

'He does,' she said tightly.

Finally the surgeon came, still dressed in his shapeless operating-room garb. She stumbled up, terrified at the tired look in the man's eyes. Here it was again, the words that had ended her life with Terry. *I'm sorry. It's over.*

'How is he?' Zeb's voice, too loud in the muted waiting-room.

The surgeon rubbed his chin where a faint shadow showed he'd been too long away from his razor. 'We didn't uncover any unexpected problems. Relieved the pressure. We'll have to wait now. His condition's stabilised, but he won't be conscious for some hours.' He frowned at the three of them, then unexpectedly smiled. 'I don't think there's too much to worry about now. Why don't you go and get some sleep?'

'What about his eyes?' she asked when Zeb didn't.

'We'll have to wait and see.'

She knew she would never sleep, and Zeb must have felt the same because he said, 'Why don't we go and move the boat to the marina? Then at least we won't have to worry about that.'

They did, the three of them crossing the bay in the middle of the night, Zeb at the wheel, docking with practised ease while Serena and Keith leapt on to the wharf with the docking lines.

Then Zeb said, 'Come with us, Serena. You booked

two hotel rooms, didn't you? Keith and I will share one. The other is for you.'

She packed her bag and went with them to the hotel, partly because the marina was miles distant from the hospital, but mostly because if she could not be with Neil she wanted to be with the people he loved.

Zeb called the hospital from the hotel, but there was no change. Neil was 'comfortable', not expected to wake until the next morning. So they all went to bed, and somehow Serena slept, feeling odd in a normal bed, alone in a hotel room. She didn't know if Zeb and Keith slept or not, but when she joined them in the lobby the next morning they both looked rested.

'Breakfast first,' Zeb insisted. 'I called the hospital and they say he was awake briefly, but he's sleeping now.'

She did not want to eat, but Zeb ordered bacon and eggs for them all; when she smelled the food, she realised that she had not eaten since yesterday morning.

At the hospital, Zeb managed to discover that Neil's eyes were bandaged and would remain so until the inflammation from the surgery and the injury subsided. It would be several days before anyone knew if he could see, but he had regained consciousness and everyone was smiling at that.

Finally, late in the morning, a nurse led them into Neil's room. He was lying in the hospital bed, bandaged, his face still terribly pale. She touched his fingers where they lay on the covers, and his hand gripped hers, hard.

'Serena,' he said, his voice warm, then his fingers released her hand and he seemed to stiffen. She felt as if he were shutting her out. 'Zeb?' His voice sounded odd and she stepped back from him.

'That's right.' Zeb touched his brother's shoulder. 'I hear you've been getting yourself into trouble again.'

Serena relaxed, seeing Neil's weak smile. 'You came to straighten me out, did you?' His voice was a little husky as he grumbled, 'By the time a fellow's thirty-eight, he should be able to escape his big brother's influence.'

'Dream on,' said Zeb, and Neil actually laughed. Then Zeb said, 'Keith's here,' and Neil's face stilled.

'Keith?' He held out his hand. Keith, standing at the end of the bed, seemed frozen in his place. Serena saw him swallow.

'Hi, Dad,' he mumbled stiffly.

'Hello.' Neil's voice was cold, too. Didn't he realise that Keith was trying to hide his uncomfortable feelings, that he cared terribly about his father lying helplessly in that bed?

The silence grew heavy. Serena touched Keith's arm. He looked at her, bit his lip, then turned and dodged out of the room. Zeb said sharply, 'Keith!'

'Don't!' Neil cleared his throat and said, 'Forget it, Zeb. Leave him alone. You shouldn't have brought him.' Neil coughed, she thought to cover his emotion. All three of them, the boy and the men, were so ridiculously masculine, so uncomfortable with the expression of their strong love for each other. Neil said now, 'You'd better see about getting him into school in San Diego.'

'We'll talk about it later,' said Zeb.

Neil said, 'There's no point. What about Mother? She didn't come, did she?'

'Are you kidding?' Zeb actually laughed. 'Mother

would have had the whole hospital in an uproar, throwing hysterics in the waiting-room, demanding a doctor to tend to her. If she was here, you'd know it. You'll be glad to know that Mother's in Phoenix, and I don't have a telephone number for her. So by the time she turns up you should be out of hospital.'

'Good,' said Neil, obviously relieved. 'What about the marina? Any problems while I've been gone?'

Serena moved restlessly. Keith was outside somewhere, angrily hurt. Neil was hurt at Keith's exit and hiding it, hiding any sign of worry about his own uncertain medical future. And now the two men were talking business!

'Nothing significant.' Zeb was saying. 'I've talked to Carlos every day on the phone, and the worst problem so far is that the slips are all full and the installation of the new moorings is behind schedule.'

'I expected that.' Neil shifted on the pillow, his fingers going to the bandages, then dropping away. 'I'll get on to that when I get back. They'll be in by the time the sailors start arriving in January. Then, hopefully, I'll be able to get those new slips in and the boatyard operating before next fall. As soon as I get out of here I'll head home and get things back on schedule. I'll leave *Passagemaker* here in San Francisco and——'

'First,' said Zeb insistently, 'you've got to come to San Diego for our general meeting.' Serena moved restlessly to the window. She couldn't believe this! Business! Details that did not matter, might never matter! Zeb was saying, 'I need you there. If you want the funds for that boatyard, I need you at our annual general meeting, or Barry will mess us all up. He wants us to declare all the profits from the Mexican operation as dividends.'

'I'll give you my proxy,' said Neil.

Zeb said, 'We'll talk about it later. Right now you'd better sleep. I'll bring Keith in this afternoon to see you.'

'Don't.' Suddenly Neil sounded terribly tired. He said tonelessly, 'Let him go back to San Diego. I'm sure that's what he wants to do.' Zeb opened his lips as if to argue, then made a frustrated noise in his throat before he turned and walked out of the room.

Serena moved a step towards the bed, then stopped. She wished she could say something to clear the closed look on his face.

'Say it!' He looked angry. He took a deep breath and she could see his hands spread on the blankets in front of him. 'Serena, I know you're still there. Say whatever it is and get it over with.'

She couldn't help smiling. He sounded so much like Keith in that moment. She stepped closer. 'Can I sit down?'

'Are you afraid of me?' His lips twitched. 'I don't believe that, Serena. I don't think you're afraid of anything.'

She pulled the chair close and sat down, then somehow her hand found his and it was easier. 'How can you say that? Don't you remember what I was like when you got me out at sea? A helpless ball of sick terror.'

'No.' His fingers closed on hers. 'Sure, you were scared. And you were sick. But you coped anyway.' She shook her head. He must be remembering this with distorted glasses. 'You not only coped, you coped alone. Thank you, Serena.' His voice had softened.

'I did it because I had to. There was no choice. I was

horribly afraid.'

'Were you?' He reached and found her face, traced the fullness of her cheek. 'By the time we got in here you were as good a sailor as any. And it isn't true that you had no choice. You were a landlubber in a disaster at sea. No one had any reason to expect you to do anything. You could have given up, curled into a ball and let the fates have their way.'

'You needed me. I *couldn't* give up. Not while there was something I could try.'

'No,' he agreed, with a smile. '*You* couldn't. A lot of women would have, but not you. You're a strong lady, Serena.'

Strong? That sounded like something you said about a lonely woman. She swallowed, because it might be true. He was holding her hand now, but this conversation was the kind that led to being alone.

'How's your head?' She reached towards the bandages, stopped herself. It must hurt, and touching would only make it worse. 'Does it hurt?'

'A bit. They're keeping me doped up.' He touched the bandage at his forehead, but she noticed that his fingers were very gentle. 'It's not bad. I'm stuck with these bandages for a few days. You know that I might never see again?'

'No! No one's said that!' She calmed her voice, as she said, 'You have to wait for the inflammation to go down.' He made an impatient sound and she said urgently, 'Neil, you mustn't——'

'I mustn't be unrealistic,' he said harshly. 'That doctor is very carefully not saying that I might not see again. That—I'm sorry, Serena. I didn't mean to talk about this.'

'Why not?' She could see the answer in his face. 'What kind of an upbringing did you and Zeb have?' He looked startled and she said, 'I can guess. It's in the way you two talk about your mother. You learned the macho bit, didn't you? Strong men, weak women who shouldn't be bothered with the nasty facts of life. And now you're getting ready to tell me to go home. Aren't you?' She swallowed and tensed because she could see that she was right.

'Yes.' He shifted, sitting up a little more. She could tell how he hated being helpless. 'There's no point to your staying.'

No point, except that she loved him. She said bitterly, 'Why don't I just go to Phoenix where your mother is? I can join her and we can avoid reality together. What about Zeb and Keith? Should they leave, too? Or is it all right for the *men* in the family to stick around?'

'I don't need a bunch of people hovering around.' He turned restlessly, leaning on one elbow. 'There's nothing they can do. I'm not in danger any more or——'

'You're a selfish man.' He stiffened and she took a deep breath. 'You're pushing everyone away, everyone who cares about you. Why, Neil?' He said nothing. She stood up, moved to the window. 'I'll tell you why. You've learned to be the strong one. That's how you and Zeb grew up, isn't it? Be strong. Don't ever let anyone see your weakness. But I did, didn't I? Out there on the ocean. Only it's not weakness, it's being human, having feelings. You think you're doing something manly, sending me away. But I care about you. I want to be near, to know if you need——'

'If I need to lean on you?' He jerked his head and

she could see the flash of pain he quickly suppressed.
'I don't need to lean on anyone, Serena. I'm not
going to be an invalid like your Terry, clinging, living
life through you, sucking you dry.'

She jerked as if he had hit her. 'It wasn't like that. I
loved Terry. I wanted to look after him. We *shared*
what happened to him. We were together.' She
swung around to face him and she had a feeling that
he knew it had not been quite like that. 'What about
out there on the ocean? I was terrified and you got me
through the bad days, cooked my meals and pretended I wasn't being a fool. I leaned on you then. You
looked after me. Why shouldn't I look after you when
you need it?'

'Forever?' He bit the word out. 'I'm not going to
lean on anyone forever, Serena. I won't be a
dependant.'

'Don't be a fool!' She pushed her hands into her
jeans pockets, blinked at her tears. 'You
wouldn't—even if you can't see, you'll learn to look
after yourself. You'll—if you wanted to push me
away—if you——Why did you make love to me that
last morning on the boat?'

He shook his head. 'Why?' she demanded, but she
knew the answer. She whispered. 'You were saying
goodbye?'

'If it didn't work out—it was selfish, but I wanted
that memory of you.' His hand moved towards the
bandages, then withdrew.

'Memory? Why just a memory? When we got here,
to San Francisco, you said you wanted me to stay.'
How long? In her heart if felt like he should be with
her forever, but what had he wanted? 'A week, we
said. What happened to that?'

'You know what happened.' He turned away from

her restlessly and pushed the button that sounded the buzzer for the nurse. 'Go home, Serena. I'll get Zeb to arrange your ticket.'

She swallowed a terrible pain in her chest. 'That's it? Just—just goodbye?' She managed a laugh somehow. 'Not even a word of thanks for crewing on your boat?'

'Yes,' he agreed, but he was not smiling. 'Thanks for crewing on my boat and——' She saw his throat move, but his lips were drawn in a tight line. 'I'll call you if things work out.'

'You'll call me?' She didn't know which was winning, the anger or the pain, but her voice was rising so it must be the anger. 'You mean, you'll call if you can see, if you're OK?'

She could hardly see anything herself, could not tell his expression through the moisture welling up in her eyes. She got in a big gulp of air so that she could talk without gasping. 'You'll call if you can be the big, strong, macho fool who doesn't really need anybody?' He wasn't saying anything at all, and she was pretty sure that he wouldn't. He had called the nurse and in a moment Serena would be told to leave. She got her legs moving, and her lips. 'Don't call,' she said flatly. 'Don't call me.'

'Serena——'

'No.' She blinked away the tears. Oh, she loved him terribly, but this would never work. 'I can't get into that kind of relationship.' She gulped, then admitted, 'I don't know what you had in mind if you get your sight back. Whether it's a week in San Francisco, or something more. I—if you don't need me with you now, when you've got problems, then you don't need me at all.' She brushed angrily at the tears that insisted on flowing down her cheeks, swallowed and whispered, 'I need you. You know that, don't you? You knew it when you made love to me. I love you, Neil.' He didn't say anything, but his hand reached out and she stepped farther away from it.

'You're doing it again,' she whispered. 'Accepting my needs, but standing alone. I do love you.' The words were a little easier to say the second time. 'I—I was trying not to dream too many dreams, but I kept seeing us together. Maybe children. I've never had the change to have children. I'd have liked to have yours, ours. I—I know you never asked me, but you might have.' She sobbed, clenched her fists angrily to fight back the emotions. 'There would have been times, again and again, when I'd be weak, when I'd need to lean on you. And if—if you never turned to me, never shared your needs with me, I'd be the one needing and needing, always taking and never able to give.

His words were stiff, perhaps concealing emotion. 'Not now, Serena. Let me get through this, then——'

She pushed her hair back, then destroyed its order in one wild shake of her head. 'I'm not a child, Neil. I'm a woman. and I don't want another father. I have one already. I want a partner, someone to stand beside me, not over me. I *don't* need someone to protect me from the facts of life. Damn it! *You're* the one who said I was strong! *Let* me be strong. Let me help. It doesn't mean you're weak.'

She could hear the swish of the nurse's rubber shoes outside the door. Neil was silent, stubbornly silent. She resisted an impulse to go to him, touch his hand, make him communicate with her. This was uncomfortably like angry sessions with her own father.

He spoke finally. 'See Zeb about your ticket, Serena. We'll——'

'We won't talk about it another time!' The nurse stopped, frozen, and Serena said quickly, angrily, 'You're treating me just like Keith, Neil, and you're wrong with both of us. You're going to lose your son if you don't reach out and tell him that you love him. You're waiting for him to make the motion, but he's too young and mixed up. If you want to keep him, you're going to have to give up that protective wall and let him know you care, even let him know that he can hurt you.'

What about her? Did he care about her? She swallowed, realised how close she was to begging for his love and managed to make herself whisper, 'Goodbye, Neil,' before she walked out of the door and out of his life.

CHAPTER NINE

SERENA did not leave San Francisco at once; she couldn't go without knowing that he was all right. She went to the boat, spent two days doing a spring clean that Neil would probably not appreciate. Zeb came each evening, filling her in on Neil's condition, but he was never able to say that Neil had asked for her.

On the third day he arrived smiling and announced, 'The bandages are off. He can see. Not completely clearly, but the doctors say that will clear up. If not, it's just a matter of glasses.'

'I'm glad for all of you.' She closed her eyes, then opened them and looked around at the boat. 'I'll go now. I'll go home.'

Zeb shifted uncomfortably. 'Don't do that. I haven't told him yet that you're still here.'

'Don't tell him.' Zeb looked stubborn and she said, 'It's not going to work out, Zeb. Don't try to solve my problems.' She smiled. He was a nice man, and she wished he *could* make her life right. 'One thing—I would like to see Keith before I go.'

When she arrived at the hotel, Keith was sprawled across the bed, glowering at the television. He opened the door and went right back to his inert pose. She sat down on the other bed and stared at the screen. It was an old re-run. She thought she had seen it before, about twenty years ago. After a few minutes he twisted around and stared at her.

143

'That's a garbage programme,' he told her sulkily.
'You don't watch that junk, do you?' He glanced
from her to the television. 'You're a teacher.'

She had to smile. 'And teachers don't watch
garbage on television? You've got to be kidding! I'll
admit I'd rather curl up with a good book, but I've
spent my share of time vegetating in front of the
television. If it's good enough for you to watch, why
can't I watch it too?'

He laughed and pushed his long form erect. He
swept a nonchalant hand towards the set and missed
the 'off' switch, then had to step closer and turn it
off.

'You know, you're not bad for a teacher.' He sat
down on the bed again, bouncing slightly as if
keeping the beat of music she could not hear. 'Uncle
Zeb says Dad can see. Did you know that?'

'Yes.' She wanted to reach over and push back that
lock of hair from his forehead. She made herself be
still, not wanting to embarrass him. 'Have you been
in to see your dad today?' Keith shook his head, the
surly look returning, and Serena said softly, 'That's
not fair, is it?'

'What d'ya mean, fair?' He hadn't been expecting
that, and she had his startled attention for a moment.
She tried to make the most of it.

'He's stuck in bed. If he were up and free to move
around, you could stomp out of the room, and he
could shout after you, and the two of you could have
it out and get the fight over. As it is, you walk out of
the room and he's helpless, and he hates being
helpless, so he can't even think straight. He's just
hurt because you walked out, and angry because he
can't do anything about it.'

Keith shrugged uncomfortably. 'He's not helpless.

He—my dad wouldn't be helpless if he was flat on his back! Even if he couldn't see any more. I bet he'd go back to Mexico and run that marina better than anyone else, even blind!'

She nodded. 'He would. You and I know he would, but he doesn't. I don't think he's ever been flat on his back in hospital in all his life. Has he?'

'No.' He shook his head, then again, more positively. 'He doesn't get sick.'

'Well, it's a good thing, because he's not very good at it.' Keith grinned at that and Serena pushed her advantage. She said softly, 'Why don't you go and see him?'

He stood up, looked out the window, then at the blank television screen. 'What about you?' he asked uneasily. 'Are you coming to see him?'

She shook her head, swallowing the painful temptation. 'This scene belongs to you and your father, Keith.' She saw him take a deep breath, then shrug as if it were something he did every day. She hoped it would work out. 'Keith, if he's a bit gruff, you will try to remember that he loves you, won't you?'

'Yeah.' He rubbed his nose, stared at his oversized running shoes and said, 'I guess so.'

'Will you write to me, Keith? I'll give you my address. I'd like to hear from you.' She shouldn't have done that, asking him to write, but she thought that she was falling in love with the boy, too, and she could not seem to walk away without clinging to something of Neil's.

She refused to let Zeb take her to the airport, and of course she paid for her own ticket. When she got home she found herself leaping up every time the telephone rang, but it was not Neil calling. It never was.

She was terribly afraid that if he called or knocked on her door she would go running to him. She even found herself dreaming about it, and in some of the dreams she was the one who went to him, begging for whatever he would give her of his life.

He had said she was strong, hadn't he? And surely she was not so weak that she would beg a man who didn't want any more than the careless pleasure of her. It took a while, but she finally realised that was what it had been. They'd been attracted to each other, but Neil had not wanted a partner, or even a relationship. If he had, he would not have sent her away.

School started, and she began to fill in the empty places in her life. She had done it before, when Terry had died, and she knew the moves. Keep busy. Don't let the evenings be empty. Concentrate on the details. It was harder this time. The empty places seemed bigger, although Neil had never said he belonged in her life at all.

The computer snarled up the autumn schedule at school and Serena was down for three classes in the same period. Schedules were shuffled and somehow her grade nine French class ended up with forty-five students. The room had thirty desks. The computer shuffled again and Serena lost her spare lesson. It didn't matter. She took her marking home. There was nothing to do in the evenings, anyway. Even Diane had deserted her, spending her evenings and some of her nights in the apartment across the hallway.

'I think I'm falling in love,' her flatmate confessed, and she looked amazingly flustered, not the old calm

Diane at all.

Keith wrote her a letter late in September. He was going to school in San Diego, staying with his uncle and his grandmother, but his father was coming for Thanksgiving weekend and they were going sailing together. It seemed that *Passagemaker* was now in San Diego, although Keith did not explain how it had got there.

She tried to read between the lines, but there weren't very many lines in the letter. The last sentence told her, 'Dad and I aren't fighting any more. Well, not much, anyway. He's busy planning the new boatyard, and I've got a job there next summer, making real money!'

It seemed Neil and Keith had at least begun to make up their feud. She was glad, although she wished Keith had said more about Neil. Were his eyes all right? Had he needed glasses? How had he got *Passagemaker* to San Diego? Would he be taking it down to Mexico later? Was he lonely down there in Mexico with his son gone? Was he filling his time with the expansion of his business? Or was there a woman? It hurt thinking of him with another woman, but it hurt more to think of him alone and lonely.

She gave her advanced French students an essay assignment using the traditional topic; 'What I did on my summer holidays'. She tried not to think about her own holidays, then gave up and let herself remember, let him into her dreams at night because he simply would not stay out. A wild passage to San Francisco, a wild passage for her heart, too.

She kept having to fight back an urge to cry. When she'd lost Terry, there had been the finality of death, but this loss was harder to accept. For one thing, it made no sense to her. He did not love her, did not want her loving him. Then why had it felt so much as if he were loving her?

Sometimes she thought of writing to him. She did not know his address in Mexico, but she had Zeb's address in San Diego. It had been on Keith's letter. Surely Zeb would forward a letter for her? But what was there to say that she had not already told him? She remembered the morning he had made love to her, and there was a lesson for her there, her need and his silence.

She registered for a night course at the university and started thinking about going back to college for graduate studies. She tried to feel some enthusiasm for becoming a student again. It seemed that she should do something.

One night she dreamed vividly that she had a child, a girl baby with Neil's fair hair. The next night she dreamed that Neil was hurt, calling for her, and she could not hear him. She woke horrified and frightened, and it took days for her to convince herself that Zeb would contact her if the dream had really been true, that Keith would write and tell her.

She got a poor mark in the midterm test for her university course. It was the first time in her life that she had made a poor showing as a student. She was wallowing in her grief, a weak fool, crying for things she could not have. Strong, Neil had said, but she was not strong.

After that she worked harder at not missing him. She used some of her savings to buy a sailing dinghy, acknowledging to herself that she would not need to save for a return to university. She enjoyed teaching, but there was no real point to graduate studies unless she wanted to get into school administration. She didn't.

She got out her Spanish tapes and worked on making her Spanish fluent, and it wasn't because Neil lived in Mexico where they spoke Spanish. She loved languages, and she had had the tapes before she had ever met the man. She went to the library, took out some Spanish novels and spent her evenings reading in a foreign language when there was no night class and no marking.

She went sailing most weekends, until late October when she dumped the dinghy and spent thirty-five endless minutes in the freezing water of Victoria harbour before she was rescued and the dinghy towed in to shore. She had a terrible cold the next week, but she ignored it—until the sneezing turned to coughing and the pains in her head and her chest drove her to the doctor.

Then she missed two weeks of school while she was hospitalised. Diane came to visit her every evening, brief visits sandwiched between her work and her lover.

'Do you want me to call your mom and dad?' Diane asked on the first visit.

'No, don't! They'll be worried. Let's just leave it.' Her words were an odd echo of Neil's.

She drank the endless jugs of fluid that she was given. She behaved, lay in bed and watched daytime soap operas on the miniature television at her bed. She spent too much time thinking, and she finally decided to go to Mexico for Christmas.

Everyone went to Mexico. Why shouldn't she? She would find out exactly where he had his marina, and there would be a hotel somewhere close by in a village. It was fine to rage at Neil and say that she did not want a relationship where she was the only vulnerable one, but wasn't she doing the same thing he was, refusing to be vulnerable?

Diane came one evening and told her that she was moving out of their shared apartment. 'Across the hallway?' speculated Serena, and her cool flatmate blushed violently.

'I love him,' Diane confessed. 'I think we might even get married. Maybe.'

So Serena would be alone. The latest letter from her parents was full of their plans to move to the Maritimes. She supposed she could move to eastern Canada herself, follow them, but it would not be easy to get a job in that part of the country. The Maritime Provinces had the highest unemployment rate of the whole country.

She had no ties here, only a flatmate who was moving out and students who kept moving on to the next grade. Were there teaching jobs in Mexico for a woman who could speak four languages? Maybe that was what she should do, think about actually moving to Mexico. Then there would be time, lots of time, to get to know Neil, to work her way past that reserve. Time for him to learn to love her or, if not that, for her to simply be close to him. Could they be friends? See each other a couple of times a month and share the fringes of their lives?

Dreams. All dreams. The day she left the hospital she knew that they were only dreams, and she was not sure if she had the courage to pursue them. She went home and found that Diane had moved everything across the hallway. The apartment was Serena's alone.

She decided that she would go to visit her parents at Christmas. It had been too many months since she had seen them, and she hadn't the courage to go to Mexico.

The letter was on the kitchen table. Diane must have put it there. Serena recognised his handwriting the instant she saw it, and her heart stopped. She went and poured herself a glass of Coke and turned up the heat in the apartment. Then she took off her coat, all the time putting off opening it, not really knowing what she was afraid of, then admitting that it was quite simple. She didn't want to be hurt again. She wanted the words to be *I love you. Please come*, and she knew he had not said that. If he loved her, would he not come, or phone? Surely something more immediate than a letter. This would be something more ordinary, impersonal. But what?

She took three sips from her glass, then went for a knife to slit the envelope open because she did not want to tear it and she was putting off reading it. A letter, with something clipped in its tone. Like his son, he did not waste many words.

Serena,
  I'm sorry our week in San Francisco didn't work out. I owe you a week's holiday. Would you accept Christmas in Mexico?

Neil

Clipped to the letter was a return ticket to Mexico, and an itinerary that had been typed up by a travel agency. A return ticket.

She wished he had put the word 'love' somewhere. It was scary, thinking of getting off the plane and walking towards him, not knowing what was in his heart. Why didn't he say something, anything to give her some indication of what he really felt about her? What was this? A debt being paid? He had promised her a week in San Francisco and his conscience was bothering him?

She would go. She was scared but, whatever his reason, she was going to go. It couldn't be any more of a risk than going to sea, could it? If she had managed that, surely she could manage a week, even if he only wanted to pay a friendly debt.

Friends, and she would not say a word about love unless he did. She bit her lip and tasted her own salty blood, and wondered if he would kiss her when they met. Then she thought to look at the date and saw the letter had been written almost a month ago. She didn't know when it had arrived here at the apartment building, but he had sent it in early October, and now it was November, and by now he must think she was ignoring this invitation.

She stumbled into her bedroom for a writing pad. She put the ticket and the letter in her top drawer with her photographs. She already had every word of the letter committed to memory, and she must not misplace those tickets. She sat at the kitchen table and tried to put words on paper for him. She put the date on the top of her writing pad, then chewed on the end of her pen while she tried to decide how to address him. *Dear Neil* sounded like an ordinary letter, one she might write to anyone, and he was so much more than that to her.

What if the Post Office took a month to get the letter back to him? He would think she had not answered him at all. She'd phone him. How the devil did you call Mexico? She had heard that the telephone system was terrible there. How could she even get his number?

He was going to be in San Diego for Thanksgiving. When did the Americans celebrate Thanksgiving, anyway? She had a feeling that it was not the same weekend the Canadians used for the celebration. She

went into the hallway to look at her calendar, and
found it useless because it was printed in Vancouver
and had only Canadian holidays on it.

The doorbell rang. She went to answer it, carrying
the calendar and the unwritten letter to Neil. Diane
would know who had Thanksgiving when. Only it
wasn't Diane at the door.

Neil.

She had been desperate to locate him, but now her
throat was too full to let any words out. She just
stared at him, and her lips wouldn't even smile. He
looked wonderful: tall and big and very healthy. If
possible, his tan was darker than she remembered,
his hair even more sun-bleached.

He wasn't smiling. He was staring at her,
frowning, demanding, 'Why didn't you answer your
phone? Where have you been?'

She shook her head wordlessly and he demanded,
'What about your flatmate? You've got a flatmate,
haven't you? Where was she?'

She opened the door wider. If he was going to
shout at her, he might as well come in. She stepped
back and he followed. She heard the door shut with a
bang.

'Where's your flatmate?' he demanded again.

'She moved out. Stop shouting at me!' But she felt
like smiling. Why would he shout if she meant
nothing to him?

'I'm not shouting!'

'You are.'

He opened his mouth, closed it, and ran angry
fingers through his hair. 'I guess I was. I didn't mean
to. I didn't come here to shout at you. I've been
phoning and there was no answer. The phone
system's not too wonderful at home, so I finally flew

up to San Diego and tried from there, but there was no answer. I was worried about you.'

That sounded rather wonderful. She smiled, and said, 'Do you always shout at people when you're worried?'

'Of course not! I——' He grinned ruefully. 'Yeah, maybe I do have that tendency. I suppose that's part of my problem with Keith.'

She didn't know what to do with her hands. She rubbed them against her thighs, then crossed her arms under her breasts. 'Do you want something? Can I get you something? A drink? Coffee? Tea?'

'Yeah. Coffee, please.' He rubbed his arms with his hands. 'Do you always keep it this cold in here?'

'I turned it up. It'll be warm soon. Come into the kitchen while I make the coffee. It's warmer there.'

He followed her, looking out the window, taking in her view of a small corner of Victoria's harbour before he sat down at the table. 'About Keith,' he said when she had begun to think he would never speak. 'I want to say thank you.'

She plugged in the kettle. 'How are you and he getting on? Did you make up the fight?'

'Mostly. We're both trying pretty hard to be friends now. Thanks to you.' She shook her head, but he said, 'You talked some sense into me, and into him too, I think. I——Thanks, Serena.'

There didn't seem any more to say about that. She made the coffee and he seemed to be making a mental inventory of everything on her kitchen counters. She wondered what he thought of the mild mess of her kitchen. Did he think she was a poor housekeeper? It was true, she wasn't much of a housekeeper. If that was what he wanted, he might as well leave now.

'Did your flatmate really move out?'

'Yes. Last week.' She opened a cupboard and stretched for a packet of cookies. She didn't think Neil had a particularly sweet tooth, but just coffee seemed inadequate.

He took a cookie from the plate and ate it, then a second, proving her wrong about the sweet tooth. 'You're all alone here?'

'Yes.' She put a mug in front of him and carefully poured coffee into it. 'I'm a big girl now, you know, Neil. All grown up. It's OK for me to be living alone.' He stared at her and she said, 'I'm twenty-nine. I'll be thirty next year.'

'I'm thirty-eight,' he retorted. 'What's that got to do with anything? I don't like your living alone here.'

She licked her lips, wished she knew just where this conversation was going, then said, 'I don't like your living alone either. You are alone, aren't you? In Mexico?' For a second she was terrified he would say that there was a woman living with him, but he nodded and she felt her heart start again.

She was not sure where this was going. It seemed time for him to make some kind of declaration, to explain why he was here. For a minute she had thought that he was nervous, but she was changing her mind. There was nothing in his eyes that reached for her. She sipped her coffee and felt it scalding her tongue. It tasted awful and she hoped it was her and not the coffee. Everything had tasted odd since she had come down with pneumonia.

'You look terrible.' He put his mug down and said, 'What's happened? Where have you been?'

'In the hospital.' He went grey and she said

quickly, 'It wasn't anything. Just pneumonia.'

'Just?' He pushed his chair back and she saw the coffee slosh over the top of his cup. 'Just? People die from pneumonia, for heaven's sake! Why didn't you call me?'

'That's ridiculous!' She pushed her curls back. She was getting a headache. 'Why are you here, Neil? What do you want? You're not responsible for me. You don't owe me anything, not—not a trip to Mexico or a week in San Francisco.'

She winced at the pain over her eyes. The headache had been with her all through the cold and the pneumonia. This morning she had thought it gone, but it was pounding back now with horrible intensity. 'Will you please go away?' she whispered. She simply couldn't cope with him right now.

His hands were on her, fingers closing around her arms, and she found herself sagging, letting him draw her close against his broad chest. 'When did you get out of the hospital?'

'This afternoon.' What was he doing? 'Neil, you can't pick me up!'

'It's not hard,' he said mildly. His voice sounded right now, the Neil she remembered from those days at sea, from the party where he'd crashed his way into her heart. 'You're not very big.' He shifted her in his arms and she settled against his chest. 'Put your head down and relax,' he said, and she did, letting it rest against the strength of his shoulder. 'Where's your bedroom? I'm putting you to bed, then I'm getting a doctor.'

'It's down the hallway. On the left, I don't need a doctor. I've got one. He told me to go home and go to bed.'

'Close your eyes,' he commanded, and she smiled

because it all seemed funny. He found the right door, pushed it open and was lowering her on to her own bed before he asked softly, 'What are you laughing about?'

She giggled. 'I haven't been put to bed since I was a kid. My dad used to carry me into my room sometimes. I can just barely remember. I must have been about six. I—you're not going to undress me?'

'I'm putting you to bed. Are you up to undressing yourself?' His fingers were at the buttons of her blouse and she shrank away.

'Yes! Yes, I am!' Vaguely, she contemplated insisting that she should get up, but it seemed like a lot of work to oppose the determination in his eyes.

'Don't,' he began softly. 'Don't fight me on this, Serena.' He grinned and said softly, 'Be true to your name. Accept this serenely.' He turned and looked around, picked up a flimsy gown from the end of the bed. 'Is this what you sleep in?' She nodded, and he frowned and started rummaging through her drawers. 'This is better. You need to keep warm. Put it on while I find something for you to eat.'

'I'm not hungry,' she protested, but he ignored her. She didn't fight it. Frankly, it felt wonderful to be looked after. She pulled on her grey jogging suit, wished it were a little more feminine, and was under the covers and half alseep before he came back into the room.

'What have you been eating?' He bent over her to pull the covers higher. 'There's nothing at all in your cupboards. I'm going out to get something. You stay put and keep warm.'

Some time later she thought he fed her a mug of soup, but it might have been a dream because when he took the mug away from her his lips covered hers and he murmured, 'I've dreamed of doing this.'

Her arms found the wonderful breadth of his shoulders, and she felt her softness crushed against him for a long, sweet moment before he said, 'No. We're going to do it right this time, lovely Serena. Go to sleep.'

The words had to be a dream, because they simply didn't make sense.

CHAPTER TEN

SERENA went to sleep so quickly that he was worried. What if she was having a relapse? She looked pale and terribly weak. Neil cursed himself for not realising sooner that she was sick. Damn! He'd come in demanding answers, actually shouting at her.

It was not the way he had planned it. He had flown north telling himself that it was some mix-up that the telephone hadn't been answered for some very ordinary, very harmless reason. At one point he even told himself that she would answer the door and he'd see in her eyes everything he was looking for; then he could take her in his arms and there wouldn't be any need for difficult words.

All his life, he had managed somehow to avoid putting himself in a vulnerable position, making declarations that left him wide open. He should have known this would be different, that Serena would not simply walk into his arms.

It had been different from the moment he had seen her. He'd wanted her, and had reached for her, his mind on some simple possession, touching and making love and walking away. A week or two. Kill two birds with one stone. He's needed crew, and he had wanted the woman. He admitted to himself that it was cold-blooded, but he had allocated her the days from Victoria to San Francisco and one week more. Then he would get on with his life, deal with Keith and get back to work.

The voyage had been one shock after another. Her
seasickness. Her inexperience and fear. Her
confession that she had lied to him. He hadn't
imagined that in his wildest dreams. He should have
been angry and resentful, and he had been at first.
Then she had started to work her way deeper into his
life, into his heart. The hours at sea had seemed to
slip away and he had begun to push back the future,
not wanting the moment of parting, hardly able to
imagine it.

Love. He had known the word was there, had
approached it nervously, carefully. A week together
after the cruise. Time to find out if this was serious.
He had been scared and he'd known it. Sandra was a
long way back in his past, a commitment made in a
moment and not exactly regretted, but . . .

Then that morning, waking with the wild surge of
the boat pushing the ocean away, the wind too strong
in the sails, the main sailing dangerously by the lee.
Standing on the heaving deck, pulling, trying to get
that straining tackle to release under the stress, then a
crack, a noise that had been felt as much as heard,
and blackness.

She had seemed to grow in strength, equal to any
need. The boat. Himself, unconscious. He'd found
himself depending on her, gaining confidence in her
new strength. But it had been temporary, a matter of
a few days until he'd got medical help. He'd pushed
any other possibility away.

Until after the surgery. Then he'd had to face the
possibility that he might be blind forever, dependent,
helpless. He had been terrified it would happen like
that, had known his fear must show in his face.
Afraid, he'd pushed everyone away. Keith. Zeb.
Serena. He had wanted to reach for her as he'd heard

her walking away, had been terrified he would be lost if he did.

He had never needed anyone the way he needed her, and he was not comfortable with need. He was, frankly, frightened by her strong competence. It was all right when he was strong himself. There was a certain excitement in reaching for a woman who might resist, even if she loved him. Until she'd lashed into him there in the hospital room, it hadn't occurred to him that she could feel the same: comfortable with his need but not with her own.

He did not call when he got out of the hospital. He understood what she had asked, and it was too late. In a crazy upside-down way, if he could not share the bad times with her, he could not ask her to share the good.

He went back to Mexico. Keith stayed in San Diego, but the resentment seemed to be gone. They would spend Thanksgiving together. Keith would come home for Christmas, then for summer. He tried not to think about Serena, but it was hopeless. She had never been to the white villa he lived in, had never seen his view of the warm ocean, yet she was there in all his dreams. Why did he sit down at the breakfast table and have an urge to bring coffee for her, too?

There was lots of room in the villa, especially now that Keith was only a visitor. With his son grown, perhaps it was time to think about another family. Children. She had mentioned children that day in the hospital. There were twins in his family. He wondered what the chances were that Serena might have twins. He found himself excited at the idea. She would need help, of course. He would help. He didn't have to work as hard as he did. He could give more time to his family and——

There was no family, no Serena standing in the cockpit of his boat with her brown curls catching fire in the sun, tumbling in the wind. There was Keith, his son almost grown, and they had each other again, thanks to Serena, but the rest of Neil's life seemed emptier than it had ever been.

He wanted her. He needed her, more with each lonely evening. He worked harder, driving his employees without succeeding in forgetting her for more than a moment. He tried to tell himself that if he needed a woman he could find another, one who asked less of him.

Then he stopped fighting with himself, went to the travel agent and booked her tickets for Christmas. He wrote to her. He wrote five letters. Four of them ended up in the waste-paper bin. He mailed the fifth with the tickets, afraid as soon as it was gone that the words had not been right.

She did not answer. He counted the days it should take to reach her, added a few to allow for her postal system and his. He heard on the news that they had a postal strike in Canada, but when he tried to find out more no one seemed to know anything. He phoned the Post Office in Victoria finally, and a brusque civil servant informed him that of course they were delivering mail.

She still did not answer.

He tried to telephone her. The calls seemed to take forever to go through, and he never received an answer. If he could call the Post Office in Victoria from Mexico, why could he not call Serena Jones?

He flew to San Diego. The call went through right away, but there was no answer. He tried constantly for four days. School was in session, so she must be at home. She had to go to work, didn't she? He called in the evening. No answer. No answer in the morning when he thought she should just be getting up to go to work. No answer in the middle of the night, although he let it ring and ring and ring. The operator insisted that the number was in service.

When he got to Victoria, he dashed to her apartment and there was no one there. He came back in the evening, but there was no answer when he knocked on her door. He went down to the manager's suite, but there was no answer there either.

She had been in hospital and he hadn't known. He should have been there, looking after her, making sure the doctors were caring for her properly. Damn it! He had a right to be there, to worry about her, to share it . . .

That was what she had said, and he had sent her away. She had said she loved him, and he had heard it in her voice, but he had sent her away. What had she accused him of being. *Macho idiot*? Something like that, and she hadn't been entirely wrong, either. He was a lot more comfortable with her dependencies than with his. Maybe that explained why he had shouted at her instead of taking her in his arms when she'd opened the door to her apartment, but it certainly didn't excuse it.

He was going to make it up to her. As soon as she was better, stronger. But first she needed looking after, not talking. He got her to bed, found some soup in the corner grocery shop and brought it back for her. She drank it, holding the mug between her hands, her eyes drooping in sleep as she sipped.

When he drew the covers over her shoulders and bent down to kiss her, she wound her arms around his neck and he let himself hold her close for a minute, then pushed her away before he succumbed to the temptation to make love to her warm woman's softness.

He heard the door opening and went out to see who it was who had a key. He found himself facing a fair, tidy girl who had the look of an over-efficient housekeeper.

'Who are you?' The woman stepped closer, her voice wary and aggressive at the same time. 'What are you doing here? Where's Serena?'

'She's in bed.'

The woman's hackles seemed to subside slightly. 'You've got to be Neil,' she said. 'You're too tanned to be anyone from this part of the world. Is she feeling OK? I'm Diane. I'm Serena's flatmate—I mean, I was. She said they were letting her out today, the X-ray showed her chest clear and the fever had been down for two days now. I'm across the hall. I just came to check, to see if she needs anything.'

'There's no fever.' He frowned, trying to remember the sound of her breathing. She had seemed to be breathing deeply, quietly, and he hoped that meant that her lungs were still clear.

'Are you staying?'

He flushed at something in her eyes, but he wasn't going anywhere. 'Yes. I'll look after her.'

She stared at him for a minute, then seemed to decide that he passed whatever criteria she had. 'You'd better have my key, then, so you can get in and out. You'll let me know if there's anything I can do?'

'Yes. Thanks.' He was glad of the key, because he hadn't been able to find where Serena had put hers. He had left the door unlocked when he'd gone to the grocery shop.

She slept soundly through the night. He left her for an hour to go to his hotel and check out. When he got back he put his bag in the empty bedroom that must have belonged to Diane before she'd moved out, but he slept in a chair in Serena's room, jerking awake every time she stirred.

Her eyes were clear when she woke in the morning.

'More soup?' he asked. She shook her head, but he brought it anyway. She had to have something. 'Vitamins,' he said, taking her hand and curving it around the mug. 'Calories. You need them.'

'I'm all right. I'm better. I'm really just kind of weak, but that's all.' She accepted the soup and even managed to eat half a piece of toast when he brought it. Then she slept again.

'I've been doing nothing but sleep,' she told him groggily. 'What I need is to get up and start moving around—then my energy will come back.'

'That's nonsense.' He took the plate with the toast on it away. 'If you're sleepy, you need sleep.'

'There are crumbs in my bed.'

'I'll get rid of them.' She laughed and he moved the covers and brushed the crumbs away. He wanted to take her in his arms and hold her forever, but she needed rest. He drew the curtains and made sure she was covered and she slept again.

She ate her vegetables at suppertime, although he could not talk her into having an appetite for the sausages he'd cooked. Later, when he was sure she was wide awake, he carried her into the living-room and put her on the sofa with blankets so that they could watch television together. She laughed at Bill Cosby, then fell asleep in the middle of a game of chess that she had insisted she wanted to play.

'Don't have to look after me,' she mumbled as he carried her back to her bed.

'I want to. I love you.' She didn't hear. She was sleeping in his arms. He covered her gently and tried to still his heart's panic. What would she say when she did hear? What if she didn't love him any more? What if she never had, if her words had only been a warm woman's response to his need?

The next day he called the doctor and got him to agree that Serena should not go back to work for at least a week. He called the school and told them that their French teacher would not be back until she was completely well.

He went out to Safeway and brought back a carload of groceries. She claimed that she would never eat that much in a year.

She discovered that he was a very good cook, far better than she was. He did a good job of looking after her, but she had always known he was good at that. He asked her what movies she liked, then rented a video recorder and they watched all the *Star Wars* movies, then he even brought home several old Cary Grant movies and sat with her, watching them as if he enjoyed them too.

Sooner or later she would have to take charge of her own life, but she put the moment off, enjoying this delicious, stolen week. He never once kissed her in all those days. Even when he carried her to bed there were no caresses, nothing she could interpret as an advance.

She wished he would make some kind of advance, either verbal or physical. She would welcome either, because it was becoming painfully evident that he did not have romance in mind. She wasn't sure why he was here, but it might be something like gratitude for her looking after him out at sea. She hoped not, because if that was it they had a long way to go before there was any kind of relationship that would work.

'I'm better,' she told him one morning, resisting the drugging temptation to let this go on forever, or at least as long as he would let it. 'No one in their wildest imagination could say I'm sick any longer.'

He was standing at the window, looking at her little sliver of a view. He pushed his hands into his pockets, turned finally and faced her.

'How about dinner, then?' he asked. She wished he would smile.

'Dinner? You've given me dinner every night. And lunch. And breakfast.' She loved the way his eyes sometimes turned almost black. She stored the sight away with the other memories. For later, when he was gone.

'Dinner out, I mean.' He pushed back that stubborn lock of sun-streaked hair. 'If you're really feeling up to it. We could go to dinner. A nice restaurant. A nightclub, perhaps. Somewhere not too noisy, with soft music. We could dance.' He grinned then, finally. 'Nothing strenuous, of course.'

Soft music meant the kind of dancing where a man held a woman in his arms. Her tongue slipped out to moisten lips suddenly gone dry. 'I—all right. It's my treat, though. I'll pay.' He frowned, and she saw the shadow crossing his face, the lines deepening across his forehead. 'Neil, I can't let you do everything. You've—all week, you've looked after me. The groceries. The meals. The movies. It's my turn.'

She wished the words back. He wasn't going to accept it. She could see his frown deepening, and any second he was going to tell her to forget the whole thing. By tomorrow he'd be on a plane to Mexico and she would have blown the whole thing.

'Neil, I——' No. She couldn't. She was not a soft, pliable woman, and if she started pretending to be one there was no chance for any kind of relationship succeeding. 'Would it be so terrible, Neil, if I picked up the tab?'

He pushed the hair back again. 'Believe it or not, Serena, I've never taken—been taken out by a woman who insisted on paying.'

She swallowed. 'Well, don't you think it's time? It's not consistent to expect a woman to haul on the sails and take watches, then refuse to let her pay for dinner.'

'No.' He laughed and came close to touch a glossy curl that lay against her ear. 'No, it's not, is it?' He pushed his hand into his pocket. 'I'll pick you up at seven, shall I?'

'Pick me up?' She pushed her hands through her hair, tried to look casual. 'Aren't you staying here?' His suitcase was in Diane's old room, his razor in her bathroom.

'You don't need me here now. You're better.' He turned away and went to the window again, although he must have had that bit of water and shore memorised by now. 'I should go back to my hotel.'

She tried to tell herself that, if a woman could pilot a ship alone on the high seas, she could manage to tell a man she did not want him to take his suitcase and leave. She parted her lips, but no words came out. He turned back to her and his face was a very smooth mask, interrupted only by the lines that the sun and the wind had carved.

'I'll go and get settled, then I'll be back at seven for you.'

Perhaps he had not wanted to stay. He had come and found her ill. Being Neil, of course he had stayed to look after her, but now he wanted to get away before she held him in a trap. So he had to get his suitcase out, and himself, and dinner in some public place would be an easy way to say goodbye.

She decided to wear the dress that she had worn on that first evening. It had been too dressy for the casual cruising party, but it was right for dinner and dancing. He had wanted her that night, at the party.

She did everything she could think of to make herself desirable, to dispel the image that he must have of her as a weak convalescent. Bubble bath. Perfumed shampoo and conditioner. Manicure. She had never spent an entire afternoon getting ready for a date, but she did now.

When Diane came home from work, she went across the hallway to ask, 'Can I borrow your gold pendant? It goes with my green dress. And would you do my hair? Before seven. He's picking me up at seven.'

Diane brought her scissors and trimmed Serena's hair, then coaxed it into a smooth, wavy elegance that Serena hoped would last through the evening before it turned into disorganised curls.

'Calm down,' said Diane as she surveyed her handiwork. 'You look gorgeous. What have you got to worry about? The man's nuts about you. Don't you dare touch that hair!'

Serena jerked her hand down guiltily. 'He hasn't said anything.' She gulped. 'Oh, Diane, I've never been so terrified of a date in all my life! I love him so much!'

'Come on!' Diane frowned at Serena, touched her hair with a soft stroke of the comb. 'That's better.

You really weren't meant for such an organised look. Just a touch of the windblown effect is—— Don't be a fool, Serena. No man wet-nurses a woman for a week if he doesn't care for her.'

Didn't he? Would Neil have moved in and looked after—say Gail? Probably. Gail had been his lover, and Serena didn't even really fit into that category.

'The doorbell, Serena. Answer it.'

She smoothed suddenly damp palms on the full skirt of her dress. Maybe he hadn't liked the dress at all. It was a little frivolous, gauzy without being quite transparent, floating around her when she walked. Diane pushed her and she moved to the door, opened it, and was glad at once that she had dressed up for him.

He was wearing a suit. She'd never imagined him dressed in anything quite so civilised before, but he looked wonderful. The fair hair was brushed into submission, although already straining to assert itself and stray across his forehead. He was smiling faintly, standing not quite relaxed, one hand pushed into the pocket of his trousers, straining the fabric slightly so that she could have no doubt of his maleness.

'Hi,' she said, hearing her own breathlessness.

'Hi.' His voice was low, a little husky, as if he might be starting to catch her cold. 'Are you ready?' She nodded and he took the coat she reached for and held it for her.

Diane came forward. 'Don't keep her too late,' she said uneasily. 'She's still fragile.'

Serena heard him laugh, but she couldn't see his eyes because he was behind her, sliding the coat up her arms, settling it around her shoulders carefully. 'Hello, Diane. Don't worry. I'll look after her.'

He was good at that, although not so good at being

looked after himself. She let him hold the door for her and walked a little in front of him, deciding that she might as well accept the way he was, because she loved the man. She wasn't sure if he could accept the way *she* was, or if he wanted to.

'Are you?' he asked, his voice low behind her on the stairs. She turned to look up at him. Standing two stairs behind her, he seemed larger than ever. 'Diane says you're fragile. Are you?' He was looking down at her, something disturbing in his eyes.

She swallowed, managed, 'Sometimes I am. In some ways, but not usually.' She wasn't going to ask, then could not stop herself. 'Would you rather I were?'

He came down two steps. He was beside her. She could tilt her head back and look right into his eyes. She wished he would touch her, kiss her. He said slowly, 'I don't think I would want you any different, Serena.'

She wished she knew what he meant by that. 'You pick the place,' he said suddenly, taking her arm, urging her down the stairs. 'It's your city.'

She thought she picked well. She liked the low lighting, the small table set against a window that looked over the ocean. He was smiling as they settled into the comfortable seats and gave their drinks orders.

'In Mexico,' he told her softly, 'this place would be in the open air. You'd be able to smell the night air, to hear the waves out there.'

'In Mexico,' she retorted, 'you can probably sit outside in November without freezing.'

He grinned, admitting that. 'But there's nowhere quite as beautiful as British Columbia, you know. It's just too bad that you Canadians don't have a better climate.'

'It's how we keep the place to ourselves,' she told him with a grin. 'If we had sunshine all the time, and warm winters, we'd be overrun with you Americans.'

They sipped their drinks slowly. Serena decided that she would make hers last a long time. She wasn't sure that her head could take much alcohol yet. The piano player began to fill the air with soft, moody background music, and they talked about nothing much. The weather. The music. She told him about her sailing dinghy and he gave her some tips on avoiding capsizing it in strong winds.

It was nice, warm and close, until he leaned back and asked quietly, 'Did you ever come here with Terry?'

She was very still, trying to hear what was behind his words. 'Yes,' she said. 'We came here once.' Did he resent her bringing him to a place she had been with Terry? He said nothing and she said, 'I wasn't thinking about that when I suggested we come here. I was remembering the view of the harbour and I thought you would like that. I remembered that it was quiet, too, and I thought we might want to talk. Some places are so noisy and——'

'Tell me about Terry.' She bit her lip and he said softly, 'Please, Serena.' His hand crossed the table, took hers and stilled her uneasy mangling of her napkin.

She sighed. 'I—I try to remember the first couple of years. Remembering the last part isn't as fair to Terry. He—we met at university. We were both taking our education year at UBC, both planning to teach in high schools. He was a history major and I was studying languages. We fell in love.'

She stared at Neil's hand, felt the warm strength

of him. 'It's hard to remember it now without it
seeming kind of unreal. It was very carefree, all
dreams and plans. That's what Terry did. He was a
dreamer, and history fitted him because he could live
it in his mind. That was lucky, because later that was
all he had—dreams and fantasies.'

She bit her lip, remembered, 'His plans were very
important to him. He had it all worked out. We were
going to get married. We'd work for five years, save
our money until we could afford our own boat. He
had a friend who had a sail-boat and we were going
to spend our summers sailing. He loved reading
about the old sailing ships. He didn't know a lot
about sailing—not then—but it was his dream, and
when he met me he just fitted me into it. I wanted
children, but it didn't fit into the dream.' She smiled,
and he could see the warmth lying in her eyes. 'It was
really so important to him. We'd go crewing that fifth
year, get some experience. Then our own boat and a
year cruising. Then work a year to save money for
more cruising.'

The waiter came and Neil sent him away before he
said softly, 'And then he got sick?'

She nodded. 'We'd been married two years then.
All dreams and plans. It was kind of like living two
lives. Teaching was the real world. Home was the
fantasy one. His plans sounded so practical, but I
always felt a little removed from reality. Sometimes I
got terribly impatient, wanted to scream at him that
we should be living *now*, not putting everything off
for some future adventure that might never happen.'

'What about your dreams? What did you want?'

She curled her fingers around his, said slowly, 'I
don't know. I guess I just adopted his. It seemed to
matter so much to him. Then he got sick. It seemed

like my life was even more split then. He never gave up the fantasy, three years and—I don't know. Maybe I encouraged it, too. It was easier, I guess. I'd bring home books for him, and he'd read and plan. Later, when he couldn't, I read to him.'

She took her hand away and circled her empty glass with both hands, feeling the coolness seeping into her fingers. She whispered, 'I loved him, Neil. I cared about him, hurt for him. But it wasn't a real marriage. I don't mean physically. I mean—well, it was like living with a child. It was like being a mother, maybe. Sometimes, after he got sick, I used to think that maybe it was best that he kept on dreaming, as if it could come true. He didn't seem to suffer. There wasn't a lot of pain, and he never really faced up to what was happening to him. But if it had been me who was sick—if I had needed him to be strong, there's no way he could have done it.'

He took the glass out of her hands, held them in his. He didn't say anything, not a word, but she felt warmth flowing into her. She whispered, 'Neil, you'll think this is terrible, but—I loved him, and it hurt seeing him slipping away, but when he died it was like a weight off me.'

He squeezed her hands. 'Darling, I do understand. It's not terrible at all.' His thumbs rubbed along the backs of her hands, relaxing the tension that had built with her guilty confession. 'Dance with me? Please. I want to hold you.'

Neil led her in a slow, formless dance that was little more than a pretence at dancing. He drew her close with an arm at her back, then buried his face in her curls. 'I'm not much of a dancer,' he confessed in a low voice. 'I just want an excuse to hold you in my arms.'

'You don't need an excuse.' He didn't seem to hear. She turned her head a little, nestled closer as he moved in the gentle shuffle that almost kept time to the slow music. She let her fingers stray up into the hair that brushed his collar at the back of his neck. Her touch was hesitant at first, but he did not stiffen just held her closer. She let her head drop on to his shoulder.

His lips were close to her ear, his voice very low. 'I met Sandra at university. She was in my statistics class, having trouble with maths.' He chuckled, said fondly, 'I can't imagine why she was taking statistics, anyway. She certainly had no talent for it.' He held her a little tighter. 'We were married three weeks later.'

The music stilled, but he did not release her. They stood, swaying slightly as if the music were still playing. She leaned back a little so that she could see his face. 'You were happy together.'

'Yes.' He met her eyes, admitted, 'I'm not good at this, Serena—talking about my feelings. I had some plans, dreams, things I thought we could do.' The music came again and his feet moved, his arms guiding her. 'I was pretty young, and so was she. I thought we could leave school, do some travelling together after I graduated. I was spoiled from the money point of view. Zeb was in control of my father's business and he was already making nothing but money. The whole family leaned on him, and I was no exception. I assumed the money would be there if I wanted to take it easy for a while. Then suddenly Sandra was expecting a child, and there were other things to think about. I went to Zeb and he put me to work. Then there was Keith, and a house, and that life seemed to swallow me up.'

He was still, just swaying to the music, holding her. 'It was a good life. We were happy, Serena. I loved her, and I wouldn't pretend that I didn't. I've never said this to anyone else, but I want you to understand how I—— It was a good life, but every year it seemed to close in on me tighter. I had become an office worker, a manager, and it wasn't my style but there didn't seem to be any alternatives. I loved working with boats, around boats, but Zeb had everything going so smoothly that it was tame and boring. And Sandra had everything under control at home, our life worked out so precisely. Sometimes I felt——When we launched *Passagemaker*—it was a new design and I wanted the chance to play with it, to test it. Keith was old enough to enjoy sailing, and I thought we could break out a bit, get away from cocktail parties and Sunday dinner at my mother's. It was no good, though. Sandra hated it.' He shook his head angrily, said, 'This sounds wrong, as if I were trapped, unhappy, and it's not really true. It's just that she needed it all so badly, and any of my wild, impulsive ideas were simply impossible.'

He said carefully, 'It's probably the main reason why I haven't married again. Much as I loved her, the last few years I've been able to grow, to do things, to become my own person. I could never have started anything in Mexico if—— Oh, I could have done it, but it would have been hurting her all the way. She would have been terrified to leave that world, the people who had lived in San Diego for a hundred years or so, the good cars and the beautiful old houses. If I'd tried to make her, she would have thought I was leaving her, that I didn't love her.'

She took a very careful breath. All right. He was telling her that he did not want a commitment. So she would have to be very careful not to cling to him too much. His arms dropped away from her and she saw his eyes darken. 'Whatever I just said, I loved her very much. It was a long time before I could get myself together again when she died.'

And he was afraid of risking himself like that again. She nodded, understanding what he was not saying, then she managed to ask, 'Shall we have dinner?'

He ordered a New York steak, rare, and she decided to have lobster. When the waiter was gone, he asked her, 'Are you sure you won't let me pay for this? I can probably afford it more easily than you.'

'And you'd feel more comfortable paying?' She wanted to make him smile, to push the memories away. 'You'll have to suffer. It's good for you to learn that you can't control every situation, and I can easily afford it.''

'On a teacher's salary?' She was glad that he was laughing at her a little.

'I agree that I'm not rich, but you forget that I'm not going to have to buy any groceries for about a year. You've filled every cupboard in my apartment.'

CHAPTER ELEVEN

THEY had finished their meal before she could make herself ask the question she had to have an answer to. She put down the fork and pushed her plate away, leaned back and watched him. He'd finished eating before she had, and was holding his coffee, sipping it slowly. He had become silent as he ate, and she knew that the evening would end soon.

'Neil, when are you going back to Mexico?'

'Tuesday.' He set his cup down. 'I have to be in San Diego on Wednesday for the company's annual general meeting.'

Three days and he would be gone. She watched the waiter pour her coffee and wished they were alone. It was so hard with the table between them, other people around. 'I have to be there,' he was explaining. 'My brother Barry is going to try to mess up my plans for Mexico. Barry's kind of short-sighted. He wants everything today, and he's always putting pressure on to take money out of the company instead of reinvesting it.' Neil frowned and said, 'He's got my mother on his side this time, so neither Zeb nor I can afford to miss that meeting.' He grinned ruefully then and admitted, 'My mother's a bit terrifying as it is. She'll throw a fit about the whole thing, and Zeb and I will be the bad boys being cruel to her, regardless of the fact that reinvesting is for her benefit as well as mine.'

'I have a feeling that I wouldn't get on very well with your mother.' She shouldn't have said that. It

178

was true that every word Zeb and Neil had said about
their mother had given Serena the impression of a
clinging tyrant, but you didn't criticise a man's
mother.

Surprisingly, he laughed. 'I have an idea that if I
put you and Mother alone in a room, I'd have fire-
works pretty quickly.' He pushed his cup away and
promised, 'Don't worry. I won't put you in that
position. Are you ready to go?'

In the end, he tried to take the bill away. She
grabbed it from him and got out her Visa card
because she had not expected it would be quite *that*
much. She let him leave the tip. Then, too soon, they
were at her doorstep and she was staring at the line of
his white shirt collar on his dark neck, waiting for
him to say goodbye and knowing that she was going
to cry when she got inside her door.

'Do you want to come in for something? Coffee?
Wine?' She pushed her skirt flat along her thighs and
wondered if she had the nerve to throw herself into
his arms and kiss him the way she had been wanting
to all evening.

He pushed his hands into his pockets, then slid
them out again. 'Serena——'

'Yes?'

'I——' He stopped as he heard a door open behind
him.

She saw Diane's head pop out across the hallway.
'Oh, it's you guys. I wondered.' Neil didn't move or
say anything, and Serena wanted to push her friend
back through the door. Diane sensed her lack of
welcome and said. 'Sorry, 'Night,' and closed her
door with a slight bang.

'I will come in,' he said, pushing his hands back
into his trouser pockets. She opened the door and he

followed her in, but he didn't come much past the door. He stood in her foyer as if he was ready to leave the second he had said whatever it was.

Goodbye. That was what he wanted to say.

'I——' He cleared his throat and strode over to her bookcase. He had looked at every book in it this last week, but he looked at it again as if it were strange to him. 'I sent you some tickets to Mexico. Did you get them?'

It was the first time he had mentioned that letter, the tickets, and she had been afraid to bring the subject up. If she did not ask, he would not say he had changed his mind, and she would still be able to use the ticket. She swallowed, admitted, 'Yes. They came the day I got out of hospital. They—they're in my drawer in my bedroom. Do you——' He wasn't looking at her. She wished he would, although she was afraid. 'Did you want me to give them back to you?'

He swung around to face her, and for a second she saw something hurt and vulnerable in his face, but then it was gone. 'No, I—— Did you want to give them back?'

'No.' Heaven's, she was scared. She wished he would reach for her, but maybe he never would. She managed two steps closer, but his face was too harsh and closed for her to touch him. She whispered, 'I wanted to use them. I——' What if she said too much? In San Francisco she had said far too much, pushed feelings on him that he did not want. 'Do you want me to come?'

'Of course I want you to come!' It was an angry growl. His hand reached out, then he swung away. 'Damn it, Serena! I——' He swung back, pacing towards her as if he were just going to attack.

'This was a hell of a lot simpler when I was just trying to get you into my bed!'

Her heart was thundering and she had to talk too loudly to get her voice to work at all. 'Is that what you want? To take me to bed?' Heaven knew, she wanted it too, but she hoped desperately that it was not all.

'I've always wanted that. I—damn it, Serena!'

She felt a smile growing deep inside herself. 'You're shouting again, Neil.'

'I know.' He managed to laugh, then his hands reached for her but stopped short of touching. 'I'm not good at this, darling. It's a little bit too powerful—a lot too powerful for me to feel comfortable with it. I want to reach out, to touch you, make love and . . .' He groaned, 'Serena, I've been wanting you, needing you, for so long that I can't think straight when your eyes do that. I dream of you, touching and loving and living with you. I want you so damned badly, I'm terrified that I'll grab and take and you'll—I don't want to trap you.'

She smiled, then grinned because her smile did things to the fire in his eyes. 'Trapped by love? It sounds like a pretty nice fate.' Then her voice died to a whisper. 'If you're the one doing the loving . . . and me.' She reached out and touched his face, and she felt the muscle twitch under her fingers before he turned and kissed the fingers that had caressed him.

Then his arms went around her and he was saying huskily, 'This is new to me, my darling. No one has ever touched me where you do. It scares the hell out of me, but I need you.'

She came closer, promised, 'Then I'm here, whenever you need me.' She swallowed, then said, 'At Christmas. I'll come at Christmas.'

She felt his laughter, then his growl as he covered

her lips with his and took her in a dizzying, deep
kiss. 'Christmas is too long to wait. Even tomorrow is
too far away.' His hands smoothed the dress against
her hips, slid down to her thighs and held her close
against him. Then he was still, shuddering, quiet
until he said, 'No. No, it isn't. I think I would be
waiting in a hundred years if I thought there was a
chance you might come to me. I love you, Serena.
I've never loved anyone the way I love you.'

She thought her body was going to melt into his.
Lips, hands, flesh touching, loving, longing. Then he
was lifting her up, swinging her into his arms, and
his long legs knew the way to her bedroom. She
closed her eyes and let the dizzy ride take her,
shivering with wonderful anticipation as she felt
herself sinking into the softness of her mattress.

'You didn't have to carry me,' she whispered
huskily. 'I can walk, you know.' He was a dark
shadow over her; then he moved closer and she
could touch the hardness of his face. Then it wasn't
hard any more, but filled with love and longing and
tenderness. In a moment he would touch, and the
sharing of their bodies would be only a symbol for the
deeper sharing of their souls.

He bent and touched his lips to hers, a promise that
stirred the flames gently inside her. He withdrew
then, needing to look down on her. 'I wanted to,' he
said, his voice creating a fire inside her. 'When I hold
you in my arms and look down to see you lying
against me . . . your face against my shoulder . . .
body crushed against mine . . . it makes me——' He
broke off and his lips took hers. She strained up to
him, feeling the wonderful roughness of his fingers
as they moved gently over her neck, brushed the
folds of her gauzy dress and inflamed her breasts

without even touching.

'It makes you what?' she asked, finding the joyful courage to tease him. She twisted on the bed under him and saw his eyes blaze as they followed the thrust of her breast.

'You might not like it, but it stirs something very primeval in me.' He moulded the shape of her enticing breast and found the erect nipple through the fabric with his thumb. 'All the masculine things. Chauvinistic. The pleasure of possession . . . anticipation of possession. My strength and your weakness . . . your softness and . . .' His voice failed him as she found the shape of his male torso under the suit jacket.

'Take that off,' she whispered, 'and show me just what it is that you've been anticipating. I have a feeling that I . . . Oh, Neil!'

She didn't notice how his fingers trembled as they freed her from the soft confinement of her dress. There was only the coolness of air on her naked flesh, the heat of his touch, the warm moistness of his lips exploring and caressing.

'What feeling?' He leaned back, teasing himself as much as her, feeling the strength of this woman's power over his body and his mind.

'That I might enjoy your fantasies,' she whispered. She saw him swallow and felt the hard response of his body against hers. His voice, though, was cool—a coolness threatened by the heat in his eyes.

Then he leaned back away from her, his voice withdrawn as he asked, 'What would you say if I said I thought we should wait until we're married?'

Married? She stared at him. His fingers stroked the soft flesh of her inner thigh and she shuddered. 'Neil, I—are you serious?'

'Yes, I'm serious.' He bent closer. 'I'm a coward, darling. I was going to do this very differently. I was going to say all the words, tell you I loved you and ask you—I was going to do it all before I even kissed you, work out everything before I made love to you.' He touched her very intimately and said raggedly, 'I wasn't going to make love to you. Not yet.'

She sucked in an unsteady breath, shifted herself onto her elbow. 'Neil, do you mean to tell me that—I don't believe this! If you don't want to make love, then why are you doing that? Why—— Oh!' She swallowed and tried to get her mind around the words her lips should be saying. 'You're not going to leave me alone tonight, are you?' No, that was wrong. Those weren't the words.

His hand paused, but his lips descended and created havoc with the soft flesh exposed by the bodice of her dress. 'I can't stop, not when you make such delicious sounds, as if you loved this . . . and this . . . as if you wanted me to do this.'

She gasped softly and he said, 'I don't want to tease you, Serena. I don't know why—— No, that isn't true. I love watching you like this, feeling that I can do to you what you've done to me every moment since I first saw you.' His lips opened over hers and she gave herself to him as he groaned, 'I'm going to make love to you, make you mine. Tonight. I didn't mean that, about waiting . . . what I was serious about was marrying you.'

For a minute she thought that her heart had stopped. 'Neil, you don't have to. I didn't put that price on myself for you. I—I love you, but I don't want to——'

'Trap me?' She nodded, and he moulded the wonderful curves of her face with his hands. 'I don't want to trap you either, but it isn't going to happen. Sandra and Terry did that, but it wasn't like this, was it?' She shook her head mutely and he said, 'This is a different kind of love. More. Deeper. I felt it from the beginning, although I couldn't admit it for a long time. You're the other half of me. I don't know how it works out—you and I living at opposite ends of the continent. We'll work out the details somehow. I want to marry you because that's what I feel for you, that I belong to you no matter what happens, that you belong to me. I—it was wrong of me to send you away in San Francisco, darling.' She saw what was in his eyes and knew how hard this was for him to say, how much it meant. 'I was scared, as much of my own feelings for you as of my medical future. It took me a long time to come to terms with myself. With you.'

'I love you,' she whispered.

He kissed her eyes closed. 'I was terrified to come to you, to tell you I loved you, in case it was too late. The only thing that kept me hoping was that I couldn't believe anything that felt this powerful could be one-sided. Sometimes I feel that your mind's inside mine, as if your touch would be with me even past the grave.'

She undid the buttons of his shirt, stared up at the frowning intensity of his face, the dark tan of his chest showing through the shirt. Then she touched where her eyes could see and felt him tremble.

'If you do much more of that——'

'Promises, promises,' she said softly, letting her fingers play with the curve of his muscles, the rigid peaks of his male nipples. It was time for the words to be silenced, time for loving, for living.

'This time,' he warned her softly, 'I'm prepared.'

'Good,' she whispered. 'What are we waiting for?'

They were the last two words she managed to say for an endless, spinning eternity. He knew the secret places of her womanhood, knew the touch, the kiss, that would turn her blood to fire, her voice ragged with passion as she groaned his name. He touched the soft heat of her, and this time he did not draw back from the restless loving of her hands, the open need of her womanhood.

When neither of them could bear to wait any longer, when her touch and his had driven them both almost beyond sanity, he moved over her and she opened to him, and they were one, a spinning, pulsing thrust to fulfilment that left them both shuddering and spent in each other's arms.

'Explosive,' he managed a long time later, moving to relieve her of his weight, drawing her against his chest. 'I understand now why a man might fight a war for a woman.'

'Cleopatra?' she giggled, then turned and shaped her body to his.

'Cleopatra was nothing,' he assured her, his voice so husky that she thought she believed it. 'When are you going to marry me?'

'Today?' she suggested. Her eyes closed and she could feel sleep coming.

'Too late for today,' he murmured, shifting to bring her more comfortably against him. 'We could try for Christmas. You're coming to Mexico for Christmas, aren't you?'

'Hmm.' She twisted and found that it was possible to be closer. His hand settled on her hip and caressed it absently.

'After that——' He broke off as she tipped her head found his lips within reach. It was wonderfully exciting to know that she could make him forget the words on his lips.

'After that what?' she teased, then gasped as he drew her close. Soon there would be no words, only caresses and the sounds of love again.

'Something.' His voice was vague. 'We'll work out something. I'll fly up every time I can until—maybe I should start something here. A marina or——'

She kissed his nose, then pulled away. 'No. It's too cold for you up here. You'd never make the winters. You'd lose your tan, and you'd shiver.'

He laughed. 'Want to bet? Serena, darling . . .' She saw the movement of his throat, saw his eyes darkening as the laughter left him. 'I want to be close to you. I don't want to commute to San Diego. With you here and me in Mexico, I——'

'I've got a better solution.'

He laughed. 'Are you trying to boss me around again?'

'No—yes.' She sat up and twisted to face him, stilling his hand by holding it between both of hers. 'I've never travelled anywhere, except once. A handsome man took me on a cruise to San Francisco.' She touched him, felt his response echoing through her own body. 'If I could have my fantasy, I'd apply to be released from my teaching contract at Christmas. I'm sure that could be arranged. Then my wonderful lover would take me away to live in an exotic, foreign land where I could practice my Spanish.'

He frowned. 'You've never been there. You might not like it.'

'Maybe,' she agreed. 'I can't imagine not loving the place where you live, but maybe I won't. If that happens, we can try somewhere else.'

'All right.' He covered her lips with his, and ordered huskily, 'Now, be quiet. I'm going to make love to you again . . . and again.'

Harlequin Presents®

Coming Next Month

#1271 THE WAYWARD BRIDE Daphne Clair
Pierce Allyn claims that Trista Vandeleur is a spoiled tease. Trista believes that Pierce is using her to further his career. With misgivings, they decide to marry. Then, torn by unanswered questions, each waits for the other to tell the truth.

#1272 THE POWER AND THE PASSION Emma Darcy
Her father's warning to steer clear of the dark disturbing tycoon Danton Fayette just seems to rouse Bernadette's instinct to meet the challenge. Determined to prove her father wrong, she knows she'll somehow have to fight her attraction to Danton.

#1273 BRIDE FOR A PRICE Stephanie Howard
Olivia is shattered to learn her stepfather's will left the family business in the hands of arrogant Matthew Jordan. Olivia sets out to reclaim it for her young brother's heritage, hoping that the price Matthew demands is one that she can pay.

#1274 A SPECIAL ARRANGEMENT Madeleine Ker
Romy discovers arranged marriages still exist when Xavier de Luca blackmails her. He wants heirs for his Sicilian estate—in return he'll save Romy's father from bankruptcy. Romy's feelings for Xavier are so extreme she doubts she can cope with such an arrangement.

#1275 MAN ON THE MAKE Roberta Leigh
Mark Raynor doesn't want to play nursemaid to a poor little rich girl—Charlotte Beauville doesn't want Mark's disapproving presence spoiling her fun. But she gradually comes to realize that she can trust Mark with her life!

#1276 LOVE IN A SPIN Mary Lyons
Stephanie thinks she's put the past behind her, making a contented life for herself and her young son Adam in the Cotswold village. Then Maxim Tyler moves to the manor house in the village, and the memories—and distrust—come flooding back.

#1277 FLY LIKE AN EAGLE Sandra Marton
Peter Saxon shatters Sara's peaceful life when he makes off with jewels he's being paid to guard—and takes Sara as hostage! She knows she should try to escape, turn him in—but finds herself wanting to believe he's innocent.

#1278 WISH ON THE MOON Sally Wentworth
Skye is delighted at the chance of going to the Bahamas to be bridesmaid at her cousin Jodi's wedding. Her delight changes to horror, however, when she realizes she's fallen in love with Thane Tyson—for he's the prospective groom!

Available in June wherever paperback books are sold, or through Harlequin Reader Service:

In the U.S.
901 Fuhrmann Blvd.
P.O. Box 1397
Buffalo, N.Y. 14240-1397

In Canada
P.O. Box 603
Fort Erie, Ontario
L2A 5X3

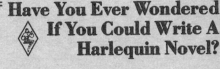

Have You Ever Wondered If You Could Write A Harlequin Novel?

Here's great news—Harlequin is offering a series of cassette tapes to help you do just that. Written by Harlequin editors, these tapes give practical advice on how to make your characters—and your story—come alive. There's a tape for each contemporary romance series Harlequin publishes.

Mail order only

All sales final

A BIG SISTER
can take her places

She likes that. Her Mom does too.

HARLEQUIN SUPPORTS BIG SISTERS
For more information, contact your local Big Brothers/Big Sisters agency.
BIG BROTHERS BIG SISTERS OF AMERICA

BIG BROTHERS/BIG SISTERS AND HARLEQUIN

Harlequin is proud to announce its official sponsorship of Big Brothers/Big Sisters of America. Look for this poster in your local Big Brothers/Big Sisters agency or call them to get one in your favorite bookstore. Love is all about sharing.

BB/BS-1A

Indulge a Little
Give a Lot

A LITTLE SELF-INDULGENCE CAN DO
A WORLD OF GOOD!

Last fall readers indulged themselves with fine romance and free gifts during the Harlequin®/Silhouette® "Indulge A Little—Give A Lot" promotion. For every specially marked book purchased, 5¢ was donated by Harlequin/Silhouette to Big Brothers/Big Sisters Programs and Services in the United States and Canada. We are pleased to announce that your participation in this unique promotion resulted in a total contribution of *$100,000.*

*

Watch for details on Harlequin® and Silhouette®'s next exciting promotion in September.

NEW COMPELLING LOVE STORIES
EVERY MONTH!

Pursuing their passionate dreams against a backdrop of the past's most colorful and dramatic moments, our vibrant heroines and dashing heroes will make history come alive for you.

HISTORY HAS NEVER BEEN
SO ROMANTIC!

Available wherever Harlequin books are sold.